W9-ARU-697

### This is Wonder.
### This is the filly I love . . .

Ashleigh's hands were shaking as she clipped a lead shank to Wonder's bridle. She quickly led the filly out the barn door. Wonder threw her head up, nearly yanking the shank from Ashleigh's hands. "Please behave, Wonder," Ashleigh pleaded. "What's wrong with you? It's just me. You've never acted liked this before. Why is she acting worse today than yesterday?" Ashleigh asked Charlie.

"Don't know. She might be in a mood. Mount up, quick."

Ashleigh panicked. "I can't do it, Charlie. I can't!"

"Yes, you can. Get up there. You gonna quit now when you're just starting? I thought you had some guts."

"I do," Ashleigh whispered.

"Then get up there. Come on, before she gets any more jittery!"

Ashleigh took a deep breath. She quickly stepped to Wonder's side, put her foot in the stirrup, gripped the base of Wonder's neck with her left hand, and swung herself up into the saddle.

## Collect all the books in the Thoroughbred series*

| | |
|---|---|
| #1 A Horse Called Wonder | #29 Melanie's Last Ride |
| #2 Wonder's Promise | #30 Dylan's Choice |
| #3 Wonder's First Race | #31 A Home for Melanie |
| #4 Wonder's Victory | #32 Cassidy's Secret |
| #5 Ashleigh's Dream | #33 Racing Parker |
| #6 Wonder's Yearling | #34 On the Track |
| #7 Samantha's Pride | #35 Dead Heat |
| #8 Sierra's Steeplechase | #36 Without Wonder |
| #9 Pride's Challenge | #37 Star in Danger |
| #10 Pride's Last Race | #38 Down to the Wire |
| #11 Wonder's Sister | #39 Living Legend |
| #12 Shining's Orphan | #40 Ultimate Risk |
| #13 Cindy's Runaway Colt | #41 Close Call |
| #14 Cindy's Glory | #42 The Bad-Luck Filly |
| #15 Glory's Triumph | #43 Fallen Star |
| #16 Glory in Danger | #44 Perfect Image |
| #17 Ashleigh's Farewell | #45 Star's Chance |
| #18 Glory's Rival | #46 Racing Image |
| #19 Cindy's Heartbreak | #47 Cindy's Desert Adventure |
| #20 Champion's Spirit | #48 Cindy's Bold Start |
| #21 Wonder's Champion | #49 Rising Star |
| #22 Arabian Challenge | #50 Team Player |
| #23 Cindy's Honor | #51 Distance Runner |
| #24 The Horse of Her Dreams | #52 Perfect Challenge |
| #25 Melanie's Treasure | #53 Derby Fever |
| #26 Sterling's Second Chance | #54 Cindy's Last Hope |
| #27 Christina's Courage | #55 Great Expectations* |
| #28 Camp Saddlebrook | |

## Collect all the books in the Ashleigh series

| | |
|---|---|
| #1 Lightning's Last Hope | #8 The Lost Foal |
| #2 A Horse for Christmas | #9 Holiday Homecoming |
| #3 Waiting for Stardust | #10 Derby Dreams |
| #4 Good-bye, Midnight Wanderer | #11 Ashleigh's Promise |
| #5 The Forbidden Stallion | #12 Winter Race Camp |
| #6 A Dangerous Ride | #13 The Prize |
| #7 Derby Day | #14 Ashleigh's Western Challenge* |

**THOROUGHBRED Super Editions**
Ashleigh's Christmas Miracle
Ashleigh's Diary
Ashleigh's Hope
Samantha's Journey

**ASHLEIGH'S Thoroughbred Collection**
Star of Shadowbrook Farm
The Forgotten Filly
Battlecry Forever!

coming soon*

# THOROUGHBRED

# WONDER'S PROMISE

## JOANNA CAMPBELL

## HarperEntertainment

*An Imprint of* HarperCollins*Publishers*

**HarperEntertainment**
*An Imprint of* HarperCollins*Publishers*
10 East 53rd Street, New York, NY 10022-5299

Produced by Daniel Weiss Associates, Inc.

HarperCollins books are available at special quantity discounts for bulk
purchases for sales promotions, premiums, or fund-raising.
For information please call or write:
Special Markets Department, HarperCollins Publishers Inc.,
10 East 53rd Street, New York, NY 10022-5299.
Telephone: (212) 207-7528. Fax: (212) 207-7222.

ISBN 0-06-051771-9

Printed in the United States of America

Visit HarperEntertainment on the World Wide Web at
www.harpercollins.com

❖ 10 9 8 7 6 5 4 3 2 1

# WONDER'S
# PROMISE

THE GRACEFUL, COPPER-COLORED THOROUGHBRED THREW UP HER head at the sound of Ashleigh Griffen's sharp whistle. The filly cantered toward the paddock fence where Ashleigh stood with her friend Linda March.

"Look at her go!" Linda cried, brushing blond curls from her cheek.

"She's looking great, isn't she?" Ashleigh said, studying the horse's elegant lines. She wasn't especially tall for a Thoroughbred, but not a midget either at fifteen hands, and she would still grow and fill out. The muscles beneath the sleek, gleaming coat were firm and well developed. Her mane and tail were long and silky. Her head was like a sculpture, with pricked ears, a wide, intelligent forehead, a slightly dished nose, and flaring nostrils. The long, seemingly fragile legs were straight and powerful.

The beautiful filly slid to a stop by the fence and

leaned her head over the rail. Ashleigh reached up and hugged her. "You're my Wonder, aren't you?" she said, planting a kiss on the filly's nose.

Wonder responded by softly nuzzling Ashleigh's dark hair, pulling it loose from its ponytail. Ashleigh carelessly tucked the hair back in place. Looking at Wonder, she felt a rush of pride. At one year and four months old, Wonder had grown into a strong and healthy horse. She'd turned out to be every bit as beautiful as Ashleigh had dreamed when she'd first set eyes on the frail, newborn foal, with her still-damp copper coat and huge, trusting eyes. Back then, no one had thought Wonder would live. And no one had thought a twelve-year-old, as Ashleigh had been then, could save her. Of course, both Wonder and Ashleigh had grown and changed a lot in the year and four months since.

"When do you think Wonder's going to go into training?" Linda asked, reaching over to rub the filly's neck. She got an affectionate nudge from Wonder in return. "My dad's already started his yearlings."

Ashleigh jerked back from her reveries. "I'm not sure." She frowned, squinting her hazel eyes. "They've started most of the yearlings already—especially the ones they've got high hopes for, like Brad Townsend's colt, Townsend Prince. Wonder's one of the last. It bothers me."

"I guess they can't start them all at once," Linda said,

understanding Ashleigh's worry. "They've got so many yearlings—over a dozen, isn't it?"

Ashleigh nodded. "I'm kind of scared about it," she admitted. "I mean, I can't wait for Wonder to start training, but you know what will happen if she doesn't do well—Mr. Townsend won't keep her on the farm. He'll send her to auction."

"She'll do okay, Ash," Linda said. "Look how she's come along. She's really got beautiful form now, and she's one of the smartest and friendliest fillies I've ever known."

"I guess I shouldn't worry so much," Ashleigh said. "Wonder is doing really well now." But Ashleigh couldn't help remembering all the struggles that had occurred during Wonder's first year of life. Ashleigh had nursed the tiny foal from birth, saving her life; then she'd nursed her again through equine influenza. But the owner of the farm, Clay Townsend, had decided Wonder was too small and too far behind the other foals to ever be a good racing prospect. He'd been ready to send Wonder off to auction. Ashleigh had had to plead for the filly, then desperately work with her to build up her weight and strength. Townsend had finally decided to keep Wonder—but only for another year. They were already six months into that year.

"And I won't be able to help with the training at all," Ashleigh added. "Mom, Dad, and Charlie have already told me that Mr. Maddock isn't going to want me interfering. I don't know how Wonder's going to act with strangers handling her. She's used to me taking care of her. Aren't you, girl?" Ashleigh turned to the horse, who was rubbing her head against Ashleigh's shoulder. Wonder answered with a low nicker.

"They let Brad help train Townsend Prince," Linda said.

Ashleigh made a face. "But Brad's the owner's son. My parents only manage the breeding stables, and they don't have anything to say about the training."

Linda sighed. "I still wouldn't get worried yet, Ash. Wonder's going to do great."

As if understanding, Wonder lifted her head and whinnied loudly.

"See?" Linda laughed.

"Yeah." Ashleigh smiled. She gave Wonder a final pat. "Linda and I are going for a ride," she told the horse. "We'll stop back later."

Wonder watched them go, then kicked up her heels and trotted to the far end of the paddock to join the other yearlings. The girls set off toward the paddock where the riding horses and Ashleigh's younger brother's pony were kept. All around them were the lush, rolling hills of Townsend Acres.

Ashleigh loved the place. She loved the sight of Thoroughbreds grazing in white-fenced paddocks, the sound of their calls, the smells of grass and fresh air and sunshine. It was early September, and the leaves would soon begin to change color. There was the end-of-summer sound of cicadas and the smell of late-cut hay. It was heaven to Ashleigh.

She hadn't felt that way when they'd first moved to Townsend Acres, though. The Griffens had had their own breeding farm before that—until a virus had swept through their barns, killing the stock. Her parents' insurance hadn't covered the losses, and they'd been forced to sell Edgardale. Ashleigh had been devastated. She'd hated having to move. She'd hated everything that had taken her away from the home she'd known! But that was in the past. After almost a year and a half, she'd gotten used to Townsend Acres—and having Wonder had helped.

Ashleigh and Linda stopped in the tack room to get saddles and bridles. The Griffens had the use of two riding horses. One was a sweet-tempered Appaloosa mare named Belle. She was a fairly big horse and had the distinctive white-and-liver spotting of the Appaloosa. The other horse, Dominator, was a retired Thoroughbred racer. He was a tall, rangy, bay gelding who'd once won major stakes races, and still had plenty of spunk. Ashleigh loved riding him. She was sure the old horse missed the excitement of his days at the track. He came to life whenever they rode through the training area, prancing like a young colt. But Belle wasn't any slouch, either. She always tried her best. She just hadn't been bred for the tremendous speed of a racing Thoroughbred.

Both Belle and Dominator trotted to the fence as the girls approached. They were expecting carrots, and they weren't disappointed.

"Hi, there, fella," Ashleigh said as Dominator lipped up his treat. "Ready to go riding?"

He snorted eagerly. Dominator was always ready to go out. Belle was anxious too, and stamped impatiently as Linda put on her saddle and fastened the cinch. The girls quickly mounted and set off at a brisk trot down one of the grassy avenues between the white-fenced pastures.

The farm stretched in every direction. Behind them were the long, low-slung breeding and yearling barns. Farther up the drive was the training area, with its own complex of stables and oval track. Beyond that were staff quarters, hay barns, and machinery sheds. All of it was surrounded by acres and acres of rolling land.

The girls took their usual route, cantering up and along the crest of the hill overlooking the farm. The view was incredible. They paused for a minute to look. Mornings were the busy time on the farm. In the training area, they could see horses being walked and cooled. Others were being exercised on the big track or in the smaller, yearling walking ring. Grooms and exercise riders moved purposefully around the stable yard.

"I really missed riding with you this summer," Linda

said as they looked down at all the activity. "Of course, going to the track with my father was fun too. Especially when one of the horses he trained won!"

"I'll bet." Ashleigh's cheeks were glowing from the fresh air, exercise, and the pure joy of being out riding. She couldn't think of anything more exhilarating, and for the moment she could forget her worries about Wonder's training. "Let's ride down to the lane and gallop them on the straight stretch. You can tell me how I'm doing."

Linda nodded eagerly, and the two girls cantered off the crest, then trotted through the patch of woods. As they came out of the woods and around a bend, they faced a long, wide, grassy stretch where the horses in training were exercised off the track. The girls pulled their horses to a stop. Ashleigh reached down and shortened her stirrups, then settled herself in a jockey's crouch high over Dominator's withers. The horse perked up his ears and snorted, knowing what was to come.

Ashleigh gripped the reins firmly in her hands, grasping a chunk of Dominator's mane as well. When she was ready, she looked over to Linda. "All set whenever you are."

Linda grinned and nodded.

"Go!" the girls cried in unison. The horses bounded forward, galloping side by side for a few seconds. Then Dominator slowly drew ahead. Ashleigh leaned low over his neck, allowing her arms and shoulders to move in rhythm with the stretching action of his stride. She loved this—the power of the horse's muscles bunching and pulling them forward, the wind whipping in her face, the sound of Dominator's snorting breaths and pounding hooves. She could hear Linda and Belle pounding along behind her.

Three-quarters of the way down the lane, Ashleigh stood slightly in the saddle and began pulling Dominator up. The old horse was enjoying the gallop as much as she and wasn't anxious to slow down, but the training yard appeared just ahead. He eased his stride down to a canter, then a trot, then Ashleigh gradually slowed him to a walk and turned him as Linda and Belle trotted up.

"Boy, you *have* gotten better over the summer!" Linda exclaimed.

"You think so?" Ashleigh said breathlessly. "Charlie's a great coach, even if he's grumpy and makes me feel like I don't know anything sometimes. You're not kidding? I looked okay?"

"You looked great. They'll be sure to let you ride Wonder after she's broken."

"I sure hope so," Ashleigh said, feeling encouraged by Linda's praise. That was her dream. That was why she'd worked so hard with the retired trainer to learn a jockey's skills. Linda wouldn't lie to her. She'd tell Ashleigh straight out if she thought Ashleigh was doing something wrong. "I've decided that when Wonder's ready, I'm going to ask Mr. Maddock if he'll watch me ride and give me a chance." Ashleigh frowned for a second. "I'm afraid he'll think I'm too young . . . and they've already got six regular exercise riders." Convincing the trainer was going to be a problem, Ashleigh knew.

The girls rode out of the lane and into the middle of the training area. A few horses were still working out on the oval, with Ken Maddock watching. Other horses were being ridden from the oval, their bodies steaming.

Ashleigh waved at the grooms and riders she knew, and got smiles in return. "There's Jilly," she said to Linda, pointing to the slim, blond woman riding out of the ring. Jilly was in her early twenties, and the only female exercise rider at the farm. Ashleigh thought she was one of the best. She handled her mounts with patience and gentleness, and Ashleigh admired that. Like Ashleigh, Jilly's goal was to be a jockey. She'd already gotten her apprentice license.

Jilly smiled as she walked her horse toward the stable. "Have a good ride?" she called.

"Great! How about you?"

Jilly gave Ashleigh a thumbs-up.

They rode on beyond the main stable area to the yearling walking ring, and drew up the horses to watch. That was where Wonder would soon start her training. Tall board fences had been built on three sides of the large dirt ring to keep the young horses from being distracted while they went through the first steps of their training. Four horses were in the ring now. Two were being circled at the end of a longe line. They worked first at a walk, then a trot, then a canter. Two were being led around the perimeter of the ring with riders in their saddles.

"That looks like Jennings, the assistant trainer, there in the red shirt," Ashleigh said, pointing to a sandy-haired man who was watching the yearlings work. "I don't know him very well—he's fairly new here—but Charlie doesn't like him much."

Linda laughed. "Charlie doesn't like a lot of people."

"That's just the way he is," Ashleigh said. "He seems grouchy all the time because he doesn't like being retired."

As she spoke, she saw the old trainer standing by the walking ring, watching. As usual, Charlie wore his rumpled felt hat and baggy clothes, and he was scowling. He looked up long enough to see Linda and Ashleigh and give them a nod—a friendly greeting for him. In a moment he walked over to the girls.

"Been out galloping?" he said, patting Dominator's sweaty shoulder. "Better cool him off good," he added to Ashleigh.

"You know I always do, Charlie."

He looked back to the ring. "Maddock's put Jennings in charge of the yearling training," he said shortly.

"He has?" Ashleigh said. Charlie didn't sound very happy about it. "You don't like what Jennings is doing with the training?" she asked.

Charlie shrugged and pursed his lips. "He seems to know his technical stuff. I'm not so sure I like his attitude."

"What do you mean?" Ashleigh looked out to where Jennings stood. He was motioning and calling instructions to one of the grooms.

"Nothing. Probably just me." With that Charlie walked off, leaving Ashleigh mystified.

Linda noticed Ashleigh's frown as the two girls rode off. "Don't get upset, Ash. You know Charlie complains all the time."

"Yeah, but he was one of the best trainers around until Mr. Townsend retired him. And I thought Mr. Maddock would be in charge of the yearling training. He can be really tough sometimes, but he knows Wonder. I don't know how Jennings will treat her."

"If he's a decent trainer, he won't be mean to her," Linda assured Ashleigh. "Maddock wouldn't hire him if he didn't know his stuff."

"Yeah, I know." Ashleigh chewed her lip. "I guess I just don't want anyone to train her but me. I keep thinking how if we still had Edgardale, we'd own all the horses. I just hate it that none of the horses here are ours—that someone else always decides what happens to them!"

"I know," Linda said. "I feel the same way about the horses my father trains. The owners don't always listen to what he thinks is best . . . and sometimes the horses get ruined because of it—overraced and stuff." Linda suddenly looked at Ashleigh and grimaced. "Oh, I shouldn't say that. I didn't mean to make you feel worse."

"No. My parents are always telling me to be realistic about Wonder. They think I've got my hopes too high. But Linda, I just know Wonder's going to be a great racehorse—no matter what anyone else thinks!"

"Well, I'm on your side," Linda said.

Ashleigh flashed her friend a grin. "Thanks."

2

LINDA LEFT LATE IN THE AFTERNOON, AFTER SHE AND ASHLEIGH had brought Wonder into the barn for the evening. Ashleigh waved good-bye to Linda, then went home to set the table for dinner. Her sister was already in the kitchen, reading a teen magazine at the table. Ashleigh stared for a second at Caroline's latest hairstyle. Caro and Rory both had their mother's fair coloring. Only Ashleigh had her father's dark hair and hazel eyes. Today Caro had pulled one side of her reddish-blond hair up on top of her head, held in place with combs. Ashleigh thought she looked like a half-clipped porcupine, but she didn't tell Caro that.

Caroline glanced up and shuddered when she saw Ashleigh's own tangled mop of dark hair, most of which had come loose from her ponytail. "You really ought to do something with your hair, Ash. And start wearing something besides jeans!"

13

"Mmm," Ashleigh said. She wasn't really listening. She'd heard it before. Caroline was always talking about clothes and hairstyles and trying to make Ashleigh over. Most of the extra allowance Caroline got for watching their eight-year-old brother, Rory, after school went toward one or the other. Ashleigh only hoped she wouldn't start acting that dumb when she was sixteen.

"Look at this," Caro said. "This hairstyle would look great on you."

Ashleigh looked over Caro's shoulder at the photo of a model with short, dark, curly hair. "Yuck! I'd look like a poodle. Besides, my hair's straight as a board."

"You could get a perm."

"No way. Move your magazine so I can set the table."

Caroline lifted her magazine a few inches so Ashleigh could slide a plate underneath. "You're really hopeless," Caroline said. "You're thirteen and a half and you still act like a complete tomboy."

"So? What's wrong with that? Linda's my age, and she's not interested in clothes and stuff either."

"Yeah, you two make a real pair."

"The horses don't care how I look, and that's what matters."

Caroline rolled her eyes, then said casually, "I haven't seen Brad Townsend around much."

"I see him all the time in the training area," Ashleigh

answered, sliding the rest of the plates around the table. She knew Caro thought Brad was cute, though she couldn't understand why. Brad was one of the biggest snobs Ashleigh had ever met. "He's going to help train Townsend Prince," Ashleigh said. "If you're so interested, you should go over and watch. Or come riding with me sometime."

Caroline flipped a page of the magazine. "Maybe I will."

Ashleigh gave her sister a startled look. Caroline hardly ever went riding. She'd learned how to ride when she was little, like Ashleigh and Rory, but she didn't really like it. She'd been afraid of riding ever since a horse had almost run away with her.

Rory burst into the kitchen. "Hi, Ashleigh!" he cried. "Will you take me riding on Moe tomorrow? Caroline doesn't want to."

"Sure," Ashleigh said, smiling at her little brother. "We'll go right after you get home from school."

Suddenly Caroline looked up from her magazine. "I've changed my mind. I'll take you after all, Rory."

Ashleigh gave her sister another startled look.

"Okay!" Rory said, satisfied. "What's for supper?"

"Spaghetti and salad," Mrs. Griffen said as she came into the kitchen. "Rory, go get washed—and comb your hair. You look like you just came through a tornado. Did you and Linda have a nice time, Ashleigh?"

"Yup. We went for a ride, and watched the yearling training for a while."

"Oh, have they started Wonder?"

"No," Ashleigh said with a frown. "I can't figure out why."

"Well, they can't do all the horses at once. Caroline, run down to the breeding barn and tell your father dinner's ready. He's in the office making out registration forms, and I think he forgot the time."

Caroline got up, taking her magazine with her. Ashleigh finished setting the table while her mother put their dinner into serving bowls.

While they were eating, Ashleigh asked her parents again about Wonder's training. "You really don't think they'll let me help?"

Her father looked up. "No, sweetheart. They've got professionals. You knew this was going to happen."

"But I know Wonder better than they do."

"That's true, but this is a business. Everyone on the farm is impressed with what you've done for Wonder, but from here on out they're looking at her as a money-earning Thoroughbred—not a pet who needs special attention."

"I don't think of her as just a pet!" Ashleigh cried. "I want her to be a fantastic racehorse, too!"

"We know," her mother added. "But Mr. Maddock knows what he's doing—he's trained racehorses for a long time."

"He's turned the yearling training over to Jennings," Ashleigh said sulkily.

"I'm sure he knows what he's doing, too," her mother said.

Ashleigh was silent for the rest of the meal, but as soon as everyone was done, she excused herself. It was Caroline's night to clean up. "I'm going down to the stables."

"Just a minute, young lady," her father said. "You spent almost the whole weekend with Linda. What about homework?"

For once Ashleigh could smile about homework. "It's done. I finished it in study hall Friday."

"All right. Just remember what happened before."

How could Ashleigh forget being grounded for months because of her lousy grades? She hadn't even been allowed to take care of Wonder. She had no intention of that happening again! "I know, Dad, and I'm doing well this year—honest."

"I certainly hope so. Don't stay out there too late."

Ashleigh hurried outside. She'd been thinking of something all afternoon, since she'd watched the yearling training. It bothered her more than she'd thought that someone else would be in charge of Wonder's training. But there was one thing she was determined to do—and that was to be the first to sit on Wonder's back.

The barn was quiet. The horses had eaten and were

dozing in their stalls. The staff had all gone to their quarters for the night. Before Ashleigh went to Wonder's stall, she collected a wooden stool that the grooms used to reach the higher shelves in the tack room. Wonder perked up and nickered as Ashleigh came to her stall door.

Ashleigh slipped into the stall. "Here, I've brought you some dessert," she said, giving Wonder some slices of apple. She ran her hand over Wonder's sleek back. "I think you're going to start your training soon," Ashleigh said.

The filly looked at her alertly, a soft, affectionate expression in her brown eyes, listening to Ashleigh's voice.

"We're going to try something new tonight," Ashleigh said. "You're going to have to get used to a saddle and someone sitting on your back pretty soon, and I think you'll feel better if I was the first one." Ashleigh hesitated. "Besides, I want to do *something* to help train you!"

Wonder nuzzled Ashleigh's palm and whoofed.

Ashleigh brought the stool into the stall. Wonder sniffed it inquisitively as Ashleigh set it down. "I just want you to get used to the weight of a rider," Ashleigh said. "All I'm going to do is lean over your back. Okay?" Wonder continued watching and listening curiously. "You know I'd never hurt you. I just need to move the stool over next to you so I can stand on it."

Ashleigh reached one hand around and moved the stool close to Wonder's side. Then she climbed up on it.

Wonder craned her head around and nudged Ashleigh with her nose. "Now I'm going to lean over your back." Ashleigh placed both her hands on the filly's smooth back. She pressed down slightly so Wonder could feel the weight. Wonder rippled her muscles but stood quietly. Ashleigh leaned farther forward, dropping her upper body over Wonder's back. The stool wobbled on the straw, and Ashleigh quickly straightened.

As she did, someone cleared his throat just outside the stall. Ashleigh froze, then looked over her shoulder. She let out a sigh of relief. "Oh, it's only you, Charlie."

"Lucky for you it is," the old man said. "If anyone else caught you trying to mount that filly—especially all by yourself in the barn—you'd be in for trouble!"

"Wonder wouldn't hurt me," Ashleigh said, patting the filly.

"Maybe not deliberately." Charlie scowled. "But she's not used to anyone hanging on her back, either. She could easily panic and throw you off. What're you trying to mount her for, anyway?"

"I wanted to get a head start on her training."

"They won't be breaking her to a rider for a while— not till she's doing okay on the longe line."

"I know, but I won't be able to help with that. I just thought it would be easier if I got her used to some of

*19*

the stuff. Getting used to a rider will be her hardest part."

"Hmph. That's what they got trainers for," Charlie said gruffly. Then his tone softened slightly. "Well, if you're so determined, at least let me hold her for you."

As he unlatched the stall door, Ashleigh flashed him a big smile. "Thanks, Charlie."

"Don't thank me. I'm probably only helping you get yourself into trouble." Wonder nudged Charlie familiarly as he took hold of her halter and rubbed her ears. They were old friends. Charlie had helped Ashleigh nurse the filly through her influenza and had given Ashleigh advice about feeding and conditioning Wonder later on, when Mr. Townsend nearly decided to sell the undersized foal. For all he'd done, though, Charlie didn't like word of it getting around the farm. He told Ashleigh that the rest of the staff would think he was getting soft and sentimental.

"Okay," Charlie said, running his hand over Wonder's neck. "Go ahead and lean your weight on her. Easy, girl," he added to the filly.

Ashleigh added her own quiet reassurance. "It's just me, girl." Carefully she slid her arms across Wonder's back and lowered the weight of her upper body. For an instant Wonder snorted in surprise. She flicked her ears forward and sidestepped nervously.

Charlie held her. "Easy now, easy." He let Wonder turn her head so that she could see it was only Ashleigh. Then Ashleigh slid forward so that she was balanced over Wonder's back on her stomach. Wonder wasn't sure what to do. She didn't like having the weight on her back, but this was her trusted friend. She pranced sideways again. Charlie tried to soothe the filly, but her movement nearly unsettled Ashleigh. Charlie grabbed Ashleigh's leg and steadied her.

"You see what could have happened if you'd done this all by yourself?" he scolded. "You would have been right off and under her feet." He calmed the nervous filly, holding her in the center of the big stall, away from the walls.

Wonder rippled her muscles uneasily and snorted, then her ears flicked back as she heard Ashleigh's voice. "Good girl," Ashleigh said quietly. "You're such a good girl." Slowly Ashleigh reached up one arm and gripped Wonder's mane in her fingers. It didn't hurt the horse. When she was sure her grip was firm, she gathered her muscles, pulled herself up, and swung her leg over Wonder's back.

Wonder flinched in surprise and swung her hindquarters around, her rear feet dancing. "It's all right . . . it's okay," Ashleigh soothed. She saw that Charlie was glaring at her. He hadn't expected her to actually sit astride the filly. He shook his head, but concentrated on quieting the nervous horse.

Ashleigh leaned over Wonder's neck, rubbing her hand over the filly's silky coat, talking softly until

Wonder slowly accepted Ashleigh's weight and finally stood still, ears flicking back and forth between Ashleigh and Charlie.

"That's enough for now," Charlie said in a moment. "Slide off her as quiet as you can."

Ashleigh did as he said. But once she had both feet firmly on the ground, she grinned broadly and went to Wonder's head. She dug a sugar cube out of her jeans pocket and fed it to the filly. "A special treat because you're such a good girl! You're terrific!"

The filly lipped up the sugar, then lifted her elegant head and nodded it decisively.

"Yeah, you know, don't you?" Ashleigh laughed. She threw her arms around Wonder's neck. "Isn't she great, Charlie?"

"You could've gotten yourself hurt," Charlie grumbled. "What if she'd reared up when you threw your leg over her?"

"She wouldn't have." Ashleigh beamed.

"You don't have enough sense to know when to be afraid," he grouched. "You haven't been around long enough to see the kind of stuff that can go wrong."

"But nothing went wrong!" Even Charlie's disapproval couldn't dim Ashleigh's spirits.

Finally Charlie relented a little. "Well, I suppose nothing did go wrong. But don't get any ideas about trying it again by yourself."

"I won't."

"Something I was going to tell you," Charlie added as he started toward the stall door. "Jennings is putting the filly in training tomorrow morning."

Ashleigh stared at Charlie, suddenly feeling a knot of panic clench her stomach. "He is?"

"Heard him talking to one of the training grooms about the schedule. You better be at the ring bright and early if you want to watch."

"But I have school tomorrow. I have to catch the bus as soon as I finish feeding Wonder!"

"I'll probably be around to keep an eye out." With that Charlie let himself out of the stall and headed out of the barn.

When he was gone, Ashleigh turned to Wonder. "Did you hear that, girl? You're going to start training."

Wonder nickered as Ashleigh laid her head against the filly's neck. Ashleigh felt a rising excitement bubbling through her. Tomorrow was going to be a big step for both of them. So much depended on Wonder's doing well in training and impressing the owner of the farm.

3

ASHLEIGH BOUNDED OUT THE FRONT DOOR OF THE HOUSE INTO the crisp morning sunshine. The sun was peeking over the horizon as she ran up the tree-lined gravel drive toward the yearling barn.

The barn was bustling with commotion. The grooms were feeding the young Thoroughbreds before leading them out to huge paddocks beyond the barns. The air echoed with the sounds of neighing horses, clattering hooves, and the distant blare of a radio playing rock music. Ashleigh said hello to the grooms as she hurried to Wonder's stall.

As she'd expected, Wonder had her head over the stall door and was looking up the aisle. When she saw Ashleigh, she let out a loud whinny.

"I'll get your breakfast right away," Ashleigh called as she hurried to the feed room. She carefully measured out Wonder's portion of grain. On the wall above was a chart, changed weekly, listing each yearling's feed schedule. Ashleigh hurried back to the stall with the bucket of grain. Wonder stepped back as Ashleigh unbolted the stall door and let herself in. As soon as Ashleigh poured the grain into the feed tray and stepped back, Wonder rushed forward and dug in.

Ashleigh patted Wonder's sleek copper-colored shoulder, glad to see that Wonder didn't seem upset by their experiment of the night before. Then she collected some brushes and lightly groomed the filly, brushing off the bits of straw that clung to her coat.

Wonder's muscles rippled in pleasure, and she looked back over her shoulder, nickering approval.

"Yeah," Ashleigh agreed, "you look good, don't you? And you'll probably go right out and roll in the mud as soon as you get in the paddock." Ashleigh swept her brush through Wonder's long, silky tail, walked forward and dropped a kiss on the filly's nose, then turned to put the brushes away.

She halted in surprise as two men suddenly walked up to Wonder's stall door. Wonder had lifted her head too, and was looking past Ashleigh's shoulder. Ashleigh recognized Jim Jennings, the assistant trainer. The muscular young man with him was one of the newer grooms from the training stables.

Ashleigh didn't know either of them except by sight, and Jennings obviously didn't recognize her. Except for a curt nod, he ignored Ashleigh and looked Wonder over. Then he spoke to the groom.

"We'll start this filly on the longe line this morning with the last bunch. Maddock tells me she was a real questionable foal last year. He doesn't think much of her potential. It'll be interesting to see how she comes along. Lead her out."

The groom nodded and went into the stall. Without a word to Ashleigh, he clipped a lead shank to Wonder's halter and started leading the filly forward. Wonder huffed nervously and swung her head to Ashleigh. She didn't understand what was going on. This man taking her shank was a stranger. The filly backed up sharply against the lead and planted her feet.

The young man gave a quick jerk on the shank. "Come on. Out of there."

Wonder wouldn't budge. She whoofed anxiously, her eyes wide.

"I'll lead her out for you," Ashleigh quickly offered. "She knows me."

"She's going to have to get used to other handlers," Jennings said shortly. He came into the stall, went to Wonder's side, and smacked her rump lightly with his hand. "Get on. Let's go! No funny business."

At his slap, Wonder jumped forward in alarm. Ashleigh's face paled. She knew the filly hated loud voices and rough handling. Jennings and the groom pulled Wonder out of the stall and down the barn aisle toward the door. The frightened filly whinnied and fought the men every inch of the way. Already her neck was darkening with a nervous sweat.

Ashleigh rushed after them, trying to do what she could. "It's all right, Wonder," she called. "There's nothing to be afraid of." Wonder flicked her ears back and calmed down for a moment at the sound of Ashleigh's familiar voice.

But Jennings called back curtly, "Let her be. I'll take care of her from here on. You must have some other work to do." He spoke to her like she was one of the hired grooms.

"You don't understand—" Ashleigh began, still following them. But they already had Wonder out of the barn and were practically dragging her up the drive toward the training area. Wonder tried to swing her head around to look for Ashleigh, but Jennings grabbed the other side of her halter, making her face forward.

Ashleigh couldn't believe what was happening—it was her worst nightmare coming true. Jennings was handling the filly all wrong. Wonder would have been fine if he'd only said a few kind words and given her a little time to get used to him and the groom.

Ashleigh looked desperately at her watch. She had only ten minutes to get to the bus. Her first instinct was to run after Wonder and forget about school. If she did, though, her parents would be furious. They understood

Ashleigh's love of horses, but were firm about the importance of school.

Ashleigh slammed her balled fist into her palm. She turned reluctantly to the house to get her backpack, then ran down the drive to wait for the bus.

Caroline was already there. "Where've you been?" she asked. "You nearly missed the bus."

"With Wonder." Ashleigh scowled.

"What are you so angry about?"

"Jennings came to get her before I left. It was awful. She was scared to death. I don't like him; he's too cold and rough. And now I have to go to school and can't even be there to calm her down!" Ashleigh cried.

"Not everyone's going to treat her like a pet the way you have," Caroline said as she brushed a piece of lint from her sleeve. "You just get too touchy about that horse sometimes."

Ashleigh glared at Caroline. "I do not! And what do *you* know, anyway?"

Caroline looked up. "Sorry!"

"Oh, forget it." Ashleigh knew Caroline would never understand her devotion to horses—and Wonder especially. Caroline just didn't feel that way. She wanted to live in a city someday and get as far away from horse farms as she could.

The bus drew up at the end of the drive and the two girls climbed on. Caroline went to sit with one of her friends, and Ashleigh slid into the seat Linda always saved for her.

"Uh-oh, what's up?" Linda said, seeing Ashleigh's expression. Quickly Ashleigh described her morning. Linda frowned when Ashleigh finished. "Maybe Charlie was right about Jennings."

"That's what I'm thinking," Ashleigh agreed. "Your father doesn't act that way with his yearlings, does he?"

"No. He says that first you've got to earn a horse's trust. But Charlie said he was going to watch the training today, didn't he?"

Ashleigh nodded. "Not that he can do much."

"At least he can tell you what happens."

"Mmm," Ashleigh said glumly.

The bus pulled up at the school complex, and Ashleigh and Linda hurried off to their lockers.

The day dragged on, and by fifth-period history class, Ashleigh wished she'd skipped school after all and taken her chances with punishment. She felt depressed as she handed in her history quiz. She'd done terribly. It wasn't that Ashleigh hadn't studied the material—she had—but her brain felt fuzzy, and she couldn't concentrate. What had happened in Wonder's first training session? She resented the fact that someone else was handling her beloved horse.

Corey Jacobs leaned over from the next desk. "You

look like you're ready to kill somebody," she said cheerfully. "You do that bad on the quiz?"

"Huh?" Ashleigh blinked and shook her head. "I was just thinking about something else."

"You're coming to pep club this afternoon, aren't you?"

"It's today? I forgot all about it. I can't come this afternoon; I have to get home."

"But today's a big game!"

Ashleigh couldn't have cared less about a football game right then. "I'll come to the next one," she said as the bell rang. "See ya later." She waved to Corey, who was looking at her like she was crazy.

Neither Caro nor Linda was on the bus after school. Caroline was getting a ride home from her friend Marcy, and Linda was staying for the game. Ashleigh remembered that they had planned to go together, but she didn't have time to find Linda and still catch the bus. She just hoped Linda wouldn't be mad.

When the bus dropped Ashleigh off, she ran straight to the yearling paddock.

Wonder was on the far side, grazing in the sunshine with some other yearlings. Ashleigh whistled. Wonder lifted her head and trotted over to the fence, but the filly seemed distracted. Instead of leaning her head over the fence as she usually did, she paced up and down.

"What's wrong?" Ashleigh asked.

Wonder only answered with a snort. She wouldn't settle down.

"It didn't go well, did it?" Ashleigh groaned. "I've got to find Charlie. I'll be back." Ashleigh reached across the fence to pat the filly, but Wonder shied away.

Ashleigh set off at a dead run up the drive toward the staff quarters. Gasping for breath, she knocked on the door of Charlie's small apartment. There was no answer. Ashleigh headed toward the stables. Charlie was sitting on a bench in the sunshine, talking to Jilly.

They both looked up and Jilly smiled. "Hi, there, Ashleigh. I see your filly went into training today."

"You were there?" Ashleigh asked.

"Only for a minute. I've been riding some two-year-olds for Maddock, and I just went by to take a look."

"She's not acting right. How'd she do?" Ashleigh asked Charlie.

Charlie resettled his floppy hat and squinted into the sun. "She was fidgety as all get out when they brought her up. She didn't seem to want any part of it. Jennings didn't look too happy."

"But Charlie, if you'd seen the way Jennings acted with her this morning. He didn't give her a chance to get used to him—just pulled her out of the stall. She was scared to death. No wonder she couldn't pay attention!"

"They're all kinda nervous at first."

31

"Maybe if I talked to Jennings and explained what Wonder's used to," Ashleigh suggested.

"Wouldn't do you any good," Charlie answered. "He's got his own ideas. And Maddock and Townsend are gone this week."

Ashleigh kicked the dirt with the toe of her sneaker. "I've got to do *something!*"

"Don't go worrying yet. Let's see how she does in the next couple days." But Charlie didn't sound very positive. "You planning on going riding today?" he added.

Ashleigh was too upset to think about riding. "I don't know."

"You're not going to do the filly any good moping around," Charlie said shortly. "Go change your clothes. I'll get the horses out and tack them up." He rose from the bench and stretched.

Ashleigh knew she'd be crazy to pass up a riding lesson from Charlie. He wasn't always in the mood to go out with her. And she was learning so much from his coaching. She gave him a weak smile. "Okay, I'll meet you at the paddock."

"If you're not doing anything," he said to Jilly, "maybe you want to come along."

Jilly shot Charlie a surprised look. Everyone knew he wasn't keen on women jockeys. He thought racing was too dangerous for women. But he liked the way Jilly handled a horse and respected her abilities—not that he'd ever tell her that to her face. Jilly's eyes brightened. "Sure, I'd love to. I'm pretty sick of cleaning tack. I'll get one of the exercise ponies."

Charlie gave a curt nod and set off toward the tack room. Jilly winked at Ashleigh. "Boy, I didn't expect that! But I'm not going to miss the chance for Charlie to give me some pointers too." Jilly paused and laid her hand on Ashleigh's shoulder. "Try not to worry too much about Wonder. She'll be okay."

Ashleigh smiled back. "I'll try."

Once they were out on the trails, Ashleigh didn't have time to think about anything except her seat in the saddle. In the cool fall air, the horses were brimming with energy and needed a firm hand on the reins. And Charlie was quick to point out any mistakes Ashleigh made.

"Get your shoulders back," he ordered, scowling at her from under the brim of his hat. "And sit down deep in that saddle. You look like a sack of grain."

Flushing, Ashleigh immediately did what she was told.

But it was such a beautiful day that the sting of Charlie's criticism didn't stay with her. Having Jilly along helped, too. When Charlie barked, Jilly glanced over at Ashleigh and grinned sympathetically, then quickly hid her smile.

As they rode three abreast in the sunshine, Ashleigh studied Jilly in the saddle. The older girl was so assured and confident, with a light touch that made riding seem effortless—and she never made any mistakes!

Ashleigh sighed in admiration. *That's how I'm going to ride one day*, she decided.

4

ASHLEIGH JUMPED UP AND CHEERED WILDLY WITH THE REST OF the pep club as the Henry Clay team scored a touchdown. The October day was overcast and cool, but that didn't bother the fans who filled the bleachers at the Saturday home game.

"Way to go!" Linda yelled from her spot beside Ashleigh. Both girls' eyes were glued to the field as their team tried for the extra point.

"Okay!" Ashleigh and Linda shouted as the football sailed between the goalposts. The touchdown and extra point had put Henry Clay into the lead in the final quarter of the game. Ashleigh was glad she'd come. She'd almost decided to stay with Wonder that day, but she knew she'd let the pep club down if she missed another game. "If we can keep going this way, we're going to win!" she cried to Linda.

"Only five more minutes," Linda said excitedly. She

passed over a bag of popcorn. "Want some?" Ashleigh shook her head and took a swallow of hot chocolate.

Out on the field, Henry Clay intercepted a pass. Bobby Starky had caught the ball and shot up the field, weaving around the opposing tackles.

Suddenly Corey Jacobs jumped to her feet on the riser behind Ashleigh. She flung up her arms and popcorn cascaded all over Ashleigh's head. "Come on, Bobby!" Corey yelled at the top of her lungs.

Ashleigh shook the kernels from her dark hair and laughed. Before the game, Corey had told them all that Bobby Starky had asked her to the movies that night. No wonder she was so excited.

Bobby raced up the field, carrying the ball toward the Henry Clay goalposts. Miraculously he escaped the tackles until he reached the twenty yard line. Then he was brought down hard.

"Oooh!" the girls moaned, but soon they were all on their feet again, cheering wildly. With the clock ticking away the last minutes of the game, the other team didn't stand a chance of scoring the tieing points. The band trumpeted, and the pep club joined the rest of the fans in yelling "Charge!"

The Henry Clay team broke from their huddle. The quarterback feinted, then passed to a receiver. He shot through the opposing line to score another touchdown! The fans went wild. The team hadn't done well that season—this was only their second win.

When the buzzer sounded, ending the game, Ashleigh's throat was sore from screaming. Corey dashed past her down the bleacher steps crying, "I've got to congratulate Bobby!"

Ashleigh and Linda grinned, then picked up the blankets they'd been sitting on and started down the bleachers with the other pep club members.

"Aren't you glad you came?" Linda asked, her voice as hoarse as Ashleigh's.

"Yeah." Ashleigh laughed. "This was fun."

The girls moved along with the crowd toward the exit. Ahead Ashleigh saw her sister and Marcy talking to some of their friends. Caro looked up and waved, and Ashleigh and Linda made their way over.

"So you guys finally won," Caroline said.

"Second time," Ashleigh answered. "I think the team's finally getting their act together. Hi, Marcy," Ashleigh added to the slim, redheaded girl standing with Caro. "You know Linda, right?"

"Sure. Hi, Linda."

"How come you guys are here?" Ashleigh asked her sister. She seriously doubted Caro and Marcy would come just to watch a middle school football game.

"We were driving by and thought you probably needed a ride," Caro said.

"Yeah, we do. We were going to call Linda's mother."

"Come on, then. Marcy's car is out in front."

The four girls weaved their way toward the parking lot.

"Thanks a lot for the ride," Linda said to Marcy. "My mom will be glad she doesn't have to drive all the way into town."

"That's okay." Marcy smiled. "I'm going to Townsend Acres anyway. Caro and I are going riding."

Ashleigh stared in amazement. "You and Caro are going riding?"

Caroline, walking ahead, turned and shrugged lazily. "I decided it was time I got over being scared."

"Oh," Ashleigh said. She gave Linda a puzzled look. "Well, that's good," she finished lamely.

They dropped Linda off at the end of her drive. "I'll talk to you tomorrow!" Ashleigh called as they drove off. As soon as Marcy had parked in the graveled lot at Townsend Acres, she and Caro jumped out of the car and headed toward the paddock where the riding horses were kept. They were talking excitedly, and Caro's voice drifted back. "If we ride on the trails behind the training stables," she said, "I'm sure we'll see Brad."

*So that's why Caro is riding again,* Ashleigh thought. *I should have guessed!* She shook her head in disgust. There were times when *she* felt like the older sister—and this was one of them. Turning on her heel, Ashleigh set off to the yearling barn to feed Wonder.

Wonder was standing in the darkest corner of the

stall. She lifted her head when Ashleigh approached with the feed pail, but there was no spark in her brown eyes. They were listless and dull, and she didn't give her usual whinny of greeting.

Ashleigh quickly unlatched the stall door, emptied the feed into Wonder's trough, then hurried over and rubbed a hand down Wonder's neck. Wonder snorted, but didn't rush over like she usually did to get her feed.

"Come on, girl," Ashleigh said, taking Wonder's halter. "I've brought your dinner. Don't you want to eat?" Ashleigh urged Wonder forward, and reluctantly the filly followed. Wonder sniffed at the grain Ashleigh had poured into her feed tray, took a mouthful, then turned away.

"You're not sick, are you?" Ashleigh asked with a frown. But Wonder didn't feel overly warm, and she wasn't acting like she was in pain. Ashleigh suspected what was wrong. Over the past week, she'd noticed a gradual change in Wonder.

"You don't like the training, do you?"

From what Charlie had told her, Ashleigh knew Wonder wasn't behaving well for Jennings. The filly was either stubborn during her training sessions or so jittery and nervous that she couldn't concentrate. She was giving Jennings every reason to think she was a dud.

"You think I'm deserting you." Ashleigh groaned. "I'd be out there with you if I could. Don't you understand, Wonder? Mr. Townsend will sell you if you don't do well in training. You'll leave the farm, and we'll never see each other again."

Suddenly Wonder lifted her head and snorted nervously. She backed rapidly across the stall and pawed the bedding with her hoof. Ashleigh went to the stall door and looked down the barn aisle. Jennings was leaving a stall at the far end, but fortunately he turned and left the barn.

Ashleigh went back to Wonder's head. "It's okay, girl. No one's coming to take you out. It's just you and me."

Wonder continued to fidget, staring toward the stall door.

Then Ashleigh heard Charlie's voice outside the stall. "Take it easy, little lady. Nothing to get upset about."

Wonder recognized him and slowly calmed down, letting Ashleigh coax her out of the corner and back to her feed. "It's not you, Charlie," Ashleigh explained. "She heard Jennings. She doesn't like him at *all.* What are we going to do?"

The old man came into the stall, shaking his head. "Nothing much we can do. If I thought Jennings was abusing her, I could put in a word to Maddock. But the filly just doesn't take to him—doesn't like his manner. The other yearlings don't seem to mind, but Wonder's got the makings of a one-girl horse."

Ashleigh bit her lip. "That's my fault. Maybe I *have*

babied her too much. Maybe everyone's right—I made a pet out of her."

"Couldn't really be helped," Charlie answered. "The filly bonded with you. She knows you saved her when she was a foal." He adjusted his hat. "I also think she's the kind of horse who just naturally responds to a feminine hand—you know, easy and gentle. She'll do something because she wants to please you, not because she thinks she has to."

That night when Ashleigh left the stall, Wonder strained her head over the stall door and seemed to give Ashleigh a mournful, accusing look. It tore Ashleigh in pieces to leave her, but she was already spending as much time with the filly as she could. She had school and homework and her chores in the house.

The next week was even worse. On Monday Ashleigh's history teacher, Mr. Parker, assigned everyone a big research project. The class groaned in unison at the Friday deadline.

"Don't sound so upset," Mr. Parker said cheerfully. "You guys have had it easy so far—and we're nearing the end of the marking period. By the way, these papers will count heavily toward your final grades."

Each student was given a different topic on the period of history they were studying—the Middle Ages. Ashleigh's topic was "Food in the Middle Ages."

"This means I'll have even less time with Wonder," Ashleigh complained to Linda at lunch. "And I *have* to get a decent grade. You know I want to try to make honors this quarter to make up for last year."

"Do you want any help with the paper?" Linda offered.

"Thanks, but I don't know how you could help. It's all research and stuff."

For the rest of the week Ashleigh spent her afternoons in the school library. She wasn't alone—most of the kids in her history class were in the library too. It was torture being away from Wonder, since she knew how much Wonder needed her right now. As she read book after book, searching for descriptions of food and diet, she found herself thinking of the filly's lack of appetite. She'd noticed during her brief visits to Wonder's stall that Wonder was growing more dejected with each passing day.

On Thursday night Ashleigh stayed up past eleven, neatly recopying her notes. She sighed with relief when she turned her paper in the next day. She'd done the best job she could and thought she should get at least a *B*. Now, at last, she could spend her weekend with Wonder and try to make up for her neglect. She'd invited Linda to come over to watch the Saturday morning training.

Ashleigh was already at the training ring the next morning when Linda pedaled up on her bike. "What a day!" Linda called happily as she jumped off the bike and leaned it against a tree.

Ashleigh nodded. The leaves were a riot of color overhead and there wasn't a cloud in the sky. It was unseasonably warm, too—an Indian summer day—and Ashleigh hadn't needed the jacket she'd brought along. But her attention was concentrated on the walking ring, where Wonder was being worked on the longe line.

"They started her with the saddle this week," Ashleigh said as Linda came up beside her. "Of course, I wasn't here. Charlie said it was a good thing I'd already gotten her used to a saddle. Jennings had a hard time as it was. Wonder's turning into a different horse, Linda. She was always so friendly and sweet, but not anymore. It's as if she's doing everything on purpose to make Jennings think she's awful. The way training is going, Jennings will probably tell Mr. Maddock and Mr. Townsend they were right to want to sell her."

"Do you think she'd be different if you worked with her?" Linda asked.

"I know she would! She'd try! I don't know what to do."

"What does Charlie say?"

"Nothing much. He doesn't seem very happy about it either."

The girls turned their attention back to the walking ring. Wonder and another yearling were being worked with saddles at the end of the longe line. Other yearlings further along in training were being led around the outside of the ring with riders in their saddles.

"There's Brad." Ashleigh pointed to the dark-haired boy on a chestnut colt. "He's riding Townsend Prince. Everyone thinks he's going to do great."

"The colt looks a lot like Wonder," Linda said.

"Well, they have the same sire, Townsend Pride." Ashleigh didn't need to tell Linda that Townsend Pride was the best stallion on the farm. When he'd raced, he'd won both the Kentucky Derby and the Preakness. He had already sired some winners.

"Brad's horse looks good," Linda said.

"Yeah." Ashleigh hated to agree. Brad always seemed to have everything go just the way he wanted. When he saw a foal he liked, his father gave him permission to train it. He exercise-rode his horses himself. Ashleigh felt incredibly jealous of Brad—she couldn't help it.

"Look." Linda pointed. "Isn't that Jilly talking to Jennings?"

Ashleigh quickly looked over to the side of the ring and nodded. "Jilly said she might be helping with the yearlings."

"They're going over to Wonder."

As the girls watched, Jilly and Jennings joined the groom who'd been working Wonder. They talked for a moment, then Jilly pulled down Wonder's stirrups.

"Oh, my gosh," Ashleigh cried, hardly believing what she was seeing. "Jennings is letting Jilly ride Wonder. Fantastic! Jilly could make a difference! She knows how to handle Wonder—and Wonder likes her."

"Okay!" Linda grinned. "Maybe things are finally going to work out."

Ashleigh watched Jilly carefully mount. Jilly was talking quietly to Wonder, and Wonder's ears flicked back, listening. Slowly Jilly lowered her weight into the saddle. For an instant Wonder tensed. She sidestepped and scooted her hindquarters around in a circle. But Jilly gently patted the filly's neck and continued to talk to her.

"Good, good," Ashleigh said under her breath. "Come on, Wonder, that's your friend Jilly. She'll treat you right."

Wonder quickly relaxed. Ashleigh let out a long sigh of relief. She hadn't realized she'd been holding her breath in fear. The filly still seemed nervous, but when Jennings walked away to the side of the ring, she calmed down further. Jilly nodded to the groom, and he started leading Wonder to the outside of the walking ring. They continued around, circling the ring. Brad and two other yearlings with riders were spaced evenly ahead of them.

Linda jabbed Ashleigh with her elbow. "Look at Brad checking Wonder out. He seems kind of surprised."

Ashleigh took her eyes from Wonder and glanced at

Brad. "That's because he's never thought Wonder would be any good. He's always told me she'd never have what it takes to make it to the track." Ashleigh stared at Wonder again. "How do you think she looks?" she asked Linda nervously.

"A lot better around Jilly. She's got a nice smooth stride when she concentrates on what she's doing."

"She's still smaller than the others," Ashleigh said. "But from what Charlie says, that doesn't always make a difference on the racetrack."

"So what do you think of Jilly up on her?" Ashleigh and Linda both jumped at the gruff voice behind them. Neither of them had noticed Charlie walk up. For a change his blue eyes were twinkling.

"You didn't have anything to do with Jilly riding Wonder, did you?" Ashleigh asked slyly.

"Me?" Charlie frowned. "Since when would Jennings listen to anything I had to say? That kid thinks he knows better than anyone."

"I'll bet you had Jilly tell him Maddock wanted her to ride Wonder," Ashleigh speculated, her hazel eyes dancing.

"Now why would I do that?" Charlie asked.

"Because you've been as worried about Wonder as I have—and you know why she's been acting up—and you know that Jilly is one of the only riders who knows how to handle her."

Charlie lifted his hat and scratched his thinning gray hair. "We just got lucky, I guess."

"I'll bet." Ashleigh laughed. "Thanks, Charlie."

"No need to thank me." He squinted out at the horses, studied Wonder for a long minute, and nodded. "Always said she had good form. Nice straight leg, well-set pasterns. I like the look of her a lot better than those other two yearlings out there."

"Townsend Prince?" Linda asked. "He looks pretty good to me."

"Naw, the other two. You see the bay's kneed-in a little—might not cause any problems. I've seen plenty of knock-kneed horses win races, but you never know. That gray colt's got a jerky, uneven movement—doesn't look like he's grown into himself yet."

"I think Jennings has noticed the difference in Wonder, too," Linda said. "See him watching them."

Ashleigh saw the assistant trainer staring across at Jilly and Wonder. He was scowling in concentration.

They stayed by the ring until Jilly dismounted. She took Wonder over to Jennings, and the two talked together for a minute. When Jilly finally led Wonder out of the walking ring toward the stable, Ashleigh rushed over.

Wonder saw her coming and whinnied. Ashleigh was smiling from ear to ear as she reached up and threw her arms around Wonder's neck. "I knew you could do it! You're such a good girl. That's the way to go! She looked so much better, Jilly," Ashleigh exclaimed. "What do you think? What did Jennings say?"

Jilly smiled. "I like her. Of course, we won't know for sure until she gets out on the track and starts running, but she's got a nice feel, and once she starts concentrating, she listens and is quick to learn."

"That's my girl, huh, Wonder!" Ashleigh beamed. "But what about Jennings?"

"Well . . ." Jilly hesitated. "He thought her behaving herself today was just a fluke."

"Oh, no."

"After a couple of days, he'll see it's not a fluke," Jilly said. "I just hope I can keep riding her through the rest of the training."

"What do you mean?" Ashleigh frowned.

"Maddock may decide to put me up in some of the late fall races. If he does, I'll be going to the track, and someone else will ride Wonder."

5

ASHLEIGH WAS WHISTLING WHEN SHE BROUGHT WONDER IN FROM the paddock on Sunday night. Already there was a difference in the filly. She pranced happily alongside Ashleigh, playfully nibbling Ashleigh's hair and butting her shoulder with her nose. Wonder had made a good start after all. Ashleigh was determined to expect the best from now on.

She looked up at Wonder and grinned. "Yeah, I'm pretty happy too. Jilly's riding you is the closest thing to my riding you. I can't wait to see you out on the training oval. You'll show them how good you are, won't you?"

But the next morning when Ashleigh went to the barn, the training groom, Tim, who had been handling Wonder in the walking ring, was already there getting ready to take Wonder from her stall.

"What are you doing?" Ashleigh asked.

Wonder saw her and whinnied. Ashleigh went into the stall and looked at the groom, waiting for his answer.

"Jennings told me to take over the morning schedule for the filly now that she's in training."

"But I've always taken care of her—everyone knows that."

The groom shrugged. "I'm just following orders. This is the way Jennings does things. You've still got the afternoon schedule."

"He's doing this with all the yearlings?"

"Yup." Tim nodded. "Look, none of the training grooms are happy about it. We got enough work to do, but that's life." He started leading Wonder out.

Wonder swung her head around and looked at Ashleigh. "It's all right, girl," Ashleigh soothed. "Go on. I'm coming with you."

Ashleigh didn't let the filly see how upset she was. As the horse and groom moved up the barn aisle, she hurried alongside and followed them to the walking ring. Jennings was talking to a couple of exercise riders. As they approached the trainer, he turned and frowned at Ashleigh.

"What are you doing here?" he asked.

Ashleigh walked toward him, feeling nervous. She quickly tried to explain the situation to him.

"Maybe you didn't know, but I've taken care of Wonder since she was a foal. She almost died—and we've got this special thing. I know she'll be more re-laxed in the morning if I keep grooming her. I'd bring her up to the walking ring—"

Jennings barely heard her out. "Look, I'm busy. Don't waste my time with something as unimportant as this. I'm trying to train racehorses, not cater to some silly whim. That filly's been turned into too much of a pet as it is."

"But—"

Jennings didn't stay to listen. "I've got work to do," he said curtly as he strode off.

Ashleigh glared after him. He'd treated her like some dumb little kid. She raced down the drive, slammed into the house and got her backpack, then ran to catch the bus.

She didn't say anything to Caroline, but as soon as she sat down next to Linda, she blurted out what had happened.

"What a jerk!" Linda said. "You're sure there's noth-ing you can do? Did you tell your parents how he talked to you?"

"I didn't have time. And I don't know what they could do. They've told me all along that I shouldn't interfere with the training. Jennings isn't hurting Won-der. He's got the right to do things the way he wants. But I can't stand it, Linda! I don't think he's a good trainer, even if Mr. Townsend and Mr. Maddock do."

"At least Jilly will be riding her."

Ashleigh sighed. "I think I'd go crazy if she wasn't."

With Jilly in the saddle, Wonder made rapid progress. Within a week Jennings had Jilly take her out to the training oval. Charlie and Ashleigh watched early on Saturday morning. Jilly was riding Wonder around the track in the company of two other yearlings.

"First thing is to get her used to the track," Charlie explained. "Get her used to working counterclockwise around the oval close to the inside rail. You need to teach them not to run in a straight line and not drift to the outside rail, to save distance."

Ashleigh studied Wonder. The filly's coat gleamed like copper and her powerful muscles showed clearly as she strode out. Jilly and the other two riders kept their mounts moving in a group around the oval. The horses were full of energy and high spirits after their night's rest in their stalls, and they pranced and shook their heads. Their breath misted in the morning air.

"They'll start working them at a trot now," Charlie said, "then work up to a canter once they're warmed up. You don't start breezing them—galloping them—until they feel real confident with the track. I used to give them a week or so."

Ashleigh leaned her arms on the rail, never taking her eyes from Wonder. "She looks good to me. Am I right?" she added a little anxiously, looking up at Charlie.

"So far, so good. We won't know though till we actually see her gallop. A horse can *look* really nice, but the test is whether they have the heart to compete—whether they want to get out there in front and win."

"Wonder's got plenty of heart and courage! I'm not worried about that."

"I'd say she had—to survive all she's been up against. But will she want to run?"

Ashleigh scowled at the old trainer. "You sound like you don't think she can do it!"

"Didn't say that, but this is a risky business. You're dealing with an animal that's got its own ideas and moods. They wake up on the wrong side of the bed, just like you do some mornings, and they don't always want to do what you think they should. There can be a lot of disappointments, and you've got to be prepared."

"But Charlie, Wonder *has* to do well."

"Don't get your hopes up so high you'll be miserable if she doesn't live up to them. She's a nice filly, but there's a dozen other nice yearlings training along with her. Not all of them will have the stuff to go to the track."

"Look at her, Charlie." Ashleigh motioned. "She's trying to get out in front already." She smiled with satisfaction. Wonder, without any urging from Jilly, was straining against the bit, trying to move ahead of the other two yearlings.

"She's giving Jilly a little fight. That's it," Charlie

muttered under his breath as he stared out at the track, "keep her steady."

Wonder got her head in front of the others and seemed content to settle down a little. Ashleigh glanced over to where Jennings stood to see his reaction. But he wasn't watching Wonder. Brad Townsend had ridden up on Townsend Prince, and the two were talking.

*Darn!* Ashleigh thought. *Jennings is missing the best part!* Brad rode onto the track and began warming up Townsend Prince at a jog. As he passed Ashleigh and Charlie, Wonder and the other yearlings came out of the turn and into the stretch toward them.

Wonder suddenly saw Townsend Prince in front of her. Ashleigh watched in amazement as, once again, the filly fought to pick up her speed. For an instant she caught Jilly by surprise, then Jilly gathered the reins and tried to steady the filly. Wonder didn't like it. She jerked up her head, sidestepped, and nearly collided with the gray yearling cantering just outside of her.

"She wants to go after Townsend Prince," Ashleigh gasped.

Charlie didn't answer. He was staring at the track. "Keep her steady. Use your hand and voice."

Of course, Jilly couldn't hear Charlie, but she seemed to know what to do on her own. The rider on the gray that Wonder had bumped yelled something to Jilly and pulled his mount up. Wonder surged past the yearling on her inside, still determined to go after Townsend

Prince, but Brad and his colt had rounded the far turn and were moving down the backstretch—out of Wonder's range of vision.

Jilly stood in her stirrups, slowing Wonder, and at the same time she turned the filly, trotting her along the outside rail in the opposite direction.

Wonder tossed her head, not happy that she'd been pulled up and turned, but now she was obeying Jilly's commands.

"Whew!" Ashleigh said.

"Not good," Charlie said.

"What do you mean?"

Charlie motioned with his head toward Jennings, who was gesturing to Jilly as she trotted toward him. Ashleigh couldn't hear what the assistant trainer was saying to Jilly, but he wasn't happy.

"All he saw was that last bit—the filly acting up," Charlie said.

"But he must have known that she only wanted to catch Townsend Prince—" Ashleigh cried.

"Don't bet on it. From where he's standing, all he could see was the fireworks."

"Jilly will explain."

"Let's hope he takes her word for it."

**6**

THE ALARM BLARED ON THE NIGHTSTAND. ASHLEIGH JERKED awake and groggily reached over to turn it off. Caroline groaned from the next bed. "Why do you have to get up so early on a day off!" She grabbed her covers and pulled them over her head.

"Sorry," Ashleigh whispered. She leaned over the side of the bed to where Linda was curled up in her sleeping bag on the bedroom floor. Linda was awake and was grinning up at her.

It was barely light beyond the bedroom windows, but Ashleigh and Linda quickly dressed and slipped from the room. The breezes on the oval always started at first light, and Wonder was doing her first work at a gallop.

"Jilly told me that Jennings thought Wonder was unpredictable and needed a firmer hand—to smack her if she pulled anything again," Ashleigh whispered as the girls went downstairs to the kitchen.

"Jilly's not going to, is she?" Linda asked.

"Not if she can help it. That's the last thing Wonder needs. But Wonder's been going okay this last week, so Jennings can't really say anything."

The two girls stopped in the kitchen long enough to grab some apples for breakfast. Ashleigh's mother was already up, starting the coffee.

"You girls off to see the training?" she asked.

"Yup," Ashleigh answered. "Wonder starts her gallops."

"Well, good luck. Let me know how it goes."

The girls hurried outside and up the drive to the yearling barn. The late October air was chilly, and Ashleigh zipped up her jacket and stuck her hands in her pockets. The sun was just rising over the horizon, but the girls could already hear the sounds of activity in the training stables—horses neighing, grooms and riders calling to each other. Most of the brightly colored leaves had fallen, and they crunched under Ashleigh and Linda's feet.

Ashleigh had hoped they'd have time to visit with Wonder before the training, but she'd already been taken from her stall. "I wonder why they took her out so early." Ashleigh frowned. "I always go to see her in the mornings. She's going to think something's wrong."

"Jilly's with her, so it should be okay," Linda reassured her.

"Yeah, I guess."

As they approached the ring, Ashleigh looked for Charlie. She knew he wouldn't miss that morning's exercise. But she didn't see him or Jilly. They headed toward the yearling stable but had only gone a few yards when they saw Wonder, her saddle in place, being led toward the ring by a training groom.

"Where's Jilly?" Linda asked.

"I don't know." Ashleigh frowned. "Usually she walks out with them. Maybe she's already at the training ring." Ashleigh and Linda followed Wonder. A group of riders and horses were standing near the entry gate, but it was hard to identify anyone in the early misty light. Then Ashleigh saw a hatted figure shuffling toward them.

The girls walked quickly toward Charlie.

"There's been some changes," he said gruffly. "Jilly won't be riding today."

Ashleigh swung toward him. "Why not?"

"Maddock wants her to ride in a race today. She left for the track late last night."

"But we talked to her last night!" Ashleigh cried. "She didn't say anything to Linda and me."

"Didn't know then. Maddock only came around after nine."

Ashleigh groaned. "Then who's riding Wonder?"

"A new fella. Only been here a couple of days. His name's Jocko. I haven't seen him ride yet, so I can't tell you much about him except that he's in tight with Jennings."

Ashleigh felt sick. Linda saw her expression and laid a hand on Ashleigh's arm. "It may be okay. Maybe he rides like Jilly."

"Not if he thinks like Jennings," Ashleigh said. She looked over to where the groom had halted Wonder. She, Linda, and Charlie moved closer for a better view. A rider stepped toward Wonder. He was thin, with muscular shoulders, and only slightly taller than a professional jockey. Jennings walked beside him.

Jocko went to Wonder's side and swung himself into the saddle. The filly snorted, sidestepped, and laid her ears flat against her head. While the groom held tight to Wonder's bridle, Jocko quickly picked up the reins and slid his feet into the stirrups. Wonder shied nervously, unsettled by this strange rider. The groom led her to the gate to the training oval.

"She's confused!" Ashleigh cried. "She doesn't understand why she has a new rider."

"She's going to have to get used to other riders in the long run," Charlie said.

Ashleigh hurried to the edge of the track as Jocko rode the filly out onto the oval. Wonder danced across the track, full of high spirits. Jocko reached around and smacked her on the rump with his crop. "Settle down," he ordered.

Wonder squealed in shock at the sting of the crop. No one had ever used one on her before. She kicked out with her hind legs and fought Jocko all the more. He reacted by smacking her again.

"No, no," Ashleigh groaned.

This time at the sting of the whip Wonder reared, trying to escape the rider on her back. Jocko hauled on her reins. Wonder's forelegs hit the ground, but as soon as they did, she kicked out with her rear legs, bucking across the track.

"Get her moving!" Jennings yelled. "Don't let her get away with that!"

Wonder was bathed in sweat. Ashleigh watched in despair as Jocko fought to bring the filly under control. He dug his heels into her sides and once again brought his whip down on her rump. Wonder shot forward, breaking into an uneven canter. Jocko kept her going around the turn and along the backstretch of the track, but it was obvious that the jockey wasn't really in control. Wonder was only moving forward to escape his whip.

Charlie and Linda had come up beside Ashleigh. "Darn fool. Doesn't have any feel for horseflesh. The filly needs a gentle hand, not rough handling!" Charlie said angrily.

The battle between Jocko and Wonder continued.

Ashleigh could see the rider was determined to have his way and show Wonder who was boss. Wonder wasn't about to give in. Ashleigh's face was chalk white as Wonder and Jocko swept past. The rider's expression was grim as he forced Wonder on. The filly was in a panic. She broke into a gallop, racing around two yearlings warming up on the track. Their riders looked over in amazement as Wonder shot past. Jocko kept the filly going, smacking her once again. The terrified horse galloped two more circuits around the oval. Charlie was groaning and shaking his head, but from what Ashleigh could see of Jennings's expression, he finally looked pleased.

Wonder's chestnut coat was white with lathered sweat by the time the exhausted filly allowed Jocko to pull her up. Ashleigh could see that Wonder no longer had the strength to fight him. He'd won the battle of wills.

Jocko walked the filly back to the gate where Jennings was standing. Wonder's eyes were wide and frightened. Her nostrils flared as she drew huge breaths into her lungs.

"Why didn't you warn me?" Jocko called furiously before Jennings said a word. "The filly's unmanageable."

"She's been babied too much," Jennings said brusquely. "I always thought so, but Maddock wanted me to put a girl rider on her. Too soft."

Ashleigh couldn't stand it a second longer. She started toward the filly, but Charlie laid a hand on her arm and shook his head.

"Don't, missy. It'll only make things worse if you try to interfere."

"But Charlie, I can't let them treat her like this! She's scared out of her mind!"

"There's nothing we can do about it now. We'll try and calm her down later when she's back at the stable."

Ashleigh's eyes were stinging with tears. Linda spoke softly. "We'll think of something, Ash. Jilly will be back, and if you and Charlie explain to the head trainer that Wonder is terrified of the whip . . ."

"Won't be able to," Charlie said shortly. "Neither Maddock nor Jilly will be back for a couple of weeks."

"No!" Ashleigh cried. "By then, Wonder will be ruined."

"The filly's got heart. She just might adjust," Charlie said. But Ashleigh could tell that he didn't believe it.

Ashleigh slammed her locker shut and turned to Linda. "It's worse than I thought it would be. Wonder doesn't trust me at all anymore."

"You're really angry, aren't you?" Linda said as the girls walked up the crowded hallway toward home-room.

"If you saw Wonder, you would be, too. Every day she gets worse. Jocko's only been riding her a week, but she's like a different horse. She's jittery, and every time she hears anyone come near her stall, she starts trembling. They're breaking her spirit, and there's nothing I can do about it!"

"Well, at least you got an *A* on your history project," Linda said, trying to cheer Ashleigh up.

"Yeah." But as hard as Ashleigh had worked for the grade, an *A* didn't seem like much consolation when Wonder was so miserable.

"Maybe you should talk to your mom and dad," Linda suggested. "I know Jennings won't listen to Charlie, but your parents know Wonder—maybe if they talked to Jennings, he'd listen to them."

Ashleigh had been thinking the same thing, although she doubted Jennings would listen to them either.

"How about if I come home with you after school today?" Linda offered.

"Would you?" Ashleigh brightened a little. "You could see Wonder yourself. No one seems to believe me when I tell them how miserable she is."

The girls squeezed through the door into homeroom. Corey immediately came over with a big grin on her face. "You guys are coming next Friday night, aren't you?"

"Friday?" Ashleigh frowned. "What's happening on Friday?"

"It's the big dance!" Corey exclaimed.

"Oh, right," Linda said. "I bet I know why you're so

excited," she teased. "Bobby asked you to go with him."

Corey grinned wider in confirmation and tossed her head. "He asked me this morning! So are you coming?"

"I am," Linda answered. "What about you, Ash?"

"I don't know." Ashleigh hesitated. "I'd forgotten all about it. I'm not exactly in the mood for dances."

"Oh, come on." Corey laughed. "It'll be great. We even have a DJ coming. Don't you get sick of hanging around horses all the time?"

"I'll see." Ashleigh shrugged.

Corey hurried off to talk to some of the other kids, and Ashleigh and Linda slid into their seats. "You should go, Ash," Linda said. "We can go together. I'll have my mom pick you up. It really should be fun."

"Maybe," Ashleigh said uncertainly. Dances made her nervous. She didn't have boyfriends, like most of the other girls—but then, neither did Linda. She'd see. Right now the most important thing was to find some way to help Wonder.

"I see what you mean," Linda said later that afternoon as the girls leaned on the paddock rail watching Wonder. Wonder had come to the rail in answer to Ashleigh's whistle, but she hadn't been able to settle down. She pranced and shied at every movement and hadn't even been interested in the carrots Ashleigh offered her.

When a car rumbled down the drive, Wonder shot off across the paddock like she'd been stung.

Linda shook her blond curls. "She's a wreck—not anything like she used to be. Let's go talk to your parents."

The girls found them in the breeding barn, checking over a mare in foal who'd been off her feed. Rory was with them, impatiently jumping up and down in the barn aisle. Caroline had gone to Marcy's after school.

"You girls don't look too happy," Mr. Griffen said as he finished with the mare and stepped outside the stall. Mrs. Griffen followed, brushing off her hands on her jeans.

"Calm down, Rory," she said.

"But I'm bored!"

"I know, but Giselle isn't feeling too good. Let's not get her excited." She turned to Ashleigh and Linda. "Why the long faces?"

Ashleigh explained.

Both her parents were frowning when she'd finished. "Are you sure you're not building things out of proportion, Ashleigh?" her father asked. "You're so attached to that filly—"

"She's not, Mr. Griffen," Linda said quickly. "I was there. It's awful."

"But I can't believe Jennings would abuse a horse."

"It's not that he's abusing her," Ashleigh admitted in all fairness. "I know the riders use whips on the other horses. But Wonder can't stand it—and Mr. Jennings and Jocko just don't understand that. The more she acts up, the harder Jocko handles her. And it's not just Wonder, because she didn't act like that with Jilly!"

Mr. Griffen ran his fingers through his hair. "I don't know what I can do, Ashleigh. I agree that some horses don't like masterful handling, but I'm not a trainer, either. I'd be sticking my nose in where it doesn't belong. The mares and foals are our responsibility. Once the yearlings leave this part of the farm, I stay out of it. Not only would Jennings wonder why I'm taking such an unusual interest in one horse, but he could get angry. And I doubt Mr. Townsend would appreciate my interference either."

"They're going to ruin her spirit!"

Her father considered. "Look, Ashleigh, I know how you're feeling, and I hate to bring up a sore subject again—but Wonder's *not* your horse. She belongs to Mr. Townsend, and he's the one who'll make the decisions. If he thinks Jennings knows what he's doing, then whether Jennings is right or wrong, that's that. It's only because you worked so hard saving the filly that you've been allowed to take such a part in raising her. She's healthy and fit now, and she's not going to be given special attention anymore. Those are the facts of life, sweetheart, and there's nothing you or I can do to change them. This is a business, and there's no room for sentimentality."

"But she'd be a good racehorse if they trained her right!" Ashleigh shot back angrily.

"That remains to be seen. I'll think about it. If I get a chance tomorrow morning, I'll watch the training." He reached down for the bucket at his feet, ending the conversation.

"You know what I think," Mrs. Griffen said quickly. "You kids should all go out for a ride. It's a nice day, and the weather's not going to be good much longer."

Ashleigh kicked the toe of her boot on the concrete floor. Her father just didn't understand how she felt, even if he said he did.

"Yeah!" Rory exclaimed. "Let's go for a ride, Ash! Moe needs exercise. Come on!"

Ashleigh looked up at Rory's excited face. Maybe a long ride would make her feel better. She glanced over at Linda. "What do you think?"

"I'd love to go riding!"

"Okay, let's go then." Rory was already bounding down the barn aisle. Ashleigh and Linda followed. "Boy, do I ever wish we'd never lost Edgardale," Ashleigh said as they left the barn. "Then at least the horses would be mine."

Mr. Griffen did find time to watch the training the next morning. Ashleigh stayed in the yearling barn, mucking out Wonder's stall. She was almost afraid to watch. But when she asked him later what he thought, she was disappointed.

"I watched Wonder's whole workout," he said, "but I couldn't honestly see anything to criticize. The filly seemed nervous going out onto the track, but she never acted up. The rider wasn't abusive. He used his whip a couple of times to get her moving, but he certainly didn't overdo it. The main thing I noticed was that the filly didn't perform."

"What do you mean?"

"She made no effort. She galloped, but her times were terrible. I could see that without actually clocking her, and when Jennings had her gallop out with a couple of the other yearlings, she just hung at the back of the pack."

"When Jilly rode her, she kept trying to get in front —she almost ran away," Ashleigh said.

"I'm just telling you what I saw," her father said, looking at her sadly. "Ashleigh, you have to face up to the fact that Wonder just doesn't have the potential to be a great racehorse—or even a mediocre one."

Ashleigh couldn't believe him. Yet when she went up to the track early the next morning before school, she saw that he was right. Wonder never once put her heart into what she was doing. She looked like a loser. Ashleigh's spirits weren't improved when she watched Brad and Townsend Prince do their gallops. Brad's colt was doing beautifully. His timings were better than those of any of the other yearlings, and Brad rode off the track grinning.

Ashleigh miserably described the scene to Linda at lunch. "But why, Linda? You've seen her run. What's happened?"

"I hope she hasn't just given up."

Ashleigh crumpled the paper with the remains of her sandwich. She'd lost her appetite. "That's what I'm afraid of."

Every morning for the next week, Ashleigh was up at the crack of dawn to spend time with Wonder before the workouts began. Wonder was pathetically glad to see her, nickering deeply, rubbing her head against Ashleigh. But all the loving hours did nothing to help Wonder in the training ring. As soon as Wonder was led out toward the ring, she became a different horse. She shied nervously when Jocko jumped in the saddle and never relaxed until she was back in her stall again.

"She doesn't seem to care," Charlie remarked. They both looked miserably at the results on Charlie's stopwatch when Wonder was clocked during her breezes.

"In early training like this, you want to see them breezing a quarter mile in about twenty-four seconds. She hasn't worked better than twenty-eight yet."

"But she could, Charlie, couldn't she?"

"It'd be nice to think so. But who knows? Jennings is right about one thing—if she's going to race, she's got to get used to more than one rider. Can't have her getting moody every time there's a jockey change—and there probably would be a few of them."

"It's not just the rider, Charlie. It's the way the rider handles her."

Charlie shoved back his hat. "Yeah. And it could be that her spirit's broken. Might make a difference if Jilly gets up on her again. If it's not too late."

7

"I THINK YOU LOOK GREAT," CAROLINE TOLD ASHLEIGH ON FRI-
day night.

Ashleigh scowled at her reflection in the bedroom
mirror. Caroline had persuaded her to wear a skirt and a
pale green sweater and had transformed Ashleigh's
dark, shoulder-length hair into a mass of curls. The
skirt and sweater made her look older somehow, Ashleigh realized, and she didn't seem as skinny as she did
in jeans. But she felt strange. "I don't even look like
*me*," she complained.

"Right." Caroline laughed. "For a change, you don't
look like a tomboy."

Linda had told Ashleigh that she was wearing a skirt
too, but still Ashleigh hesitated. "I don't think I like
these curls, either," she said, watching them bounce as
she shook her head.

"You look fine, sweetheart," Mrs. Griffen said. "Very

pretty, in fact. Honestly," she added with a grin when she saw Ashleigh's expression. "Just relax and have a good time tonight."

A horn beeped in front of the house.

"That must be Linda," Mrs. Griffen said. She leaned over and quickly kissed Ashleigh's cheek. "Now stop worrying about how you look and have fun."

Caroline stood watching with a smile as Ashleigh headed out of the bedroom and down the stairs. *Sure, Caroline can gloat,* Ashleigh thought. She'd been trying to do a make-over on Ashleigh for months.

When Ashleigh slid into the car, she saw that Linda had kept her promise and worn a skirt and sweater too.

"Boy, I don't think I've ever seen you dressed up before!" Linda exclaimed. "And that hairdo's neat."

Ashleigh touched her curls. "Caro talked me into it." Then she looked anxiously at Linda. "Are you sure—absolutely positive? I feel weird dressed like this."

Linda giggled. "I'm absolutely positive! You don't look weird at all."

Ashleigh relaxed back against the seat. With Linda's assurances, she didn't feel quite as self-conscious. Maybe the dance would be fun after all.

But her nervousness returned when they reached the school gym. Tons of kids were already there. Through the gym doors, they heard the blare of rock music and loud voices. As she and Linda moved through the crowd along the edge of the gym, Ashleigh felt like a hundred eyes were staring at her and her new look.

In the center of the floor, some kids were already up dancing. Ashleigh recognized Corey and Bobby and a couple of others from her classes. Linda saw Jennifer and Stacy near the refreshment table. "Let's go stand with them," she said, going off in that direction.

Jennifer took one look at Ashleigh and burst out, "Oh, wow, look at you!" Jennifer had huge blue eyes, masses of long blond hair, and a figure like a model in a magazine. Ashleigh couldn't tell from Jennifer's tone if her remark was a compliment or an insult, but some of the other kids started laughing. Ashleigh blushed furiously. Her hot cheeks made her even more embarrassed, but before Jennifer could say any more, Tony Vasso walked over and asked Jennifer to dance.

Within seconds Linda and Stacy were asked to dance too, then some of the other girls nearby. Ashleigh suddenly found herself standing all alone. She looked around at the girls who were left without partners and felt like crawling into a hole.

She tried to pretend it didn't matter that she was left on the sidelines. She played with the silver bracelet Caroline had coaxed her into wearing and stared off across the gym at the dancers, at the DJ, at the bright streamers hanging from the ceiling—anywhere but at the boys, who all seemed to be clustered in groups. In truth, she was so embarrassed she wanted to die.

And the evening only got worse. The DJ went from one song to the next, and still no one approached her to dance. Even Angela White, who wasn't very popular, had been asked once. Linda, Jennifer, and Stacy dashed back from time to time, but they were having so much fun, they didn't seem to notice that Ashleigh was totally alone. She gritted her teeth and kept staring blindly across the gym. The minutes dragged by like hours, and she knew her cheeks were getting redder and redder. Finally she couldn't take it anymore. She fled across the floor, ignoring everyone, and escaped to the hall outside the gym. Linda found her there a few minutes later.

"Why are you hiding out here?" Linda asked.

Ashleigh glowered. "You would too if no one asked *you* to dance."

"But I've only been dancing with Billy Mitchell— he's not exactly the greatest."

"At least he asked you! I feel like a jerk. I should never have let Caro talk me into wearing this dumb outfit and doing my hair like a poodle."

"You look fine, Ash. I think the guys aren't asking you to dance because they're afraid to."

"Afraid of me? Linda, you're losing it."

"Well, you're standing there with this awful expression on your face. You look like you'd rather beat them up than dance with them."

Ashleigh was surprised to hear this description of

herself. But she frowned fiercely again. "I hate dances. I knew I shouldn't have come!"

Linda gave up. When Ashleigh got home, she immediately doused her head under the faucet and got rid of the disgusting curls, swearing tearfully that she'd never go to another dance as long as she lived. Horses were much better company than boys!

She wasn't in any better a mood in the morning. She overslept because she'd gotten home so late, and she missed her chance to spend some time with Wonder before training. But since it was Saturday, at least she could watch the training—not that that would cheer her up.

When she approached the ring, though, she saw it wasn't going to be a regular morning. Clay Townsend and Ken Maddock were both standing beside the training oval with Jennings. Several horses were already out on the oval, and one of them was Wonder. Ashleigh's heart sank.

But if Maddock was back, then Jilly must be back. Ashleigh looked around but didn't see her. She did see Charlie and made her way toward him. It was a cold morning, and Charlie had put on his heavy jacket and had his hands stuffed in his pockets.

"What's going on?" Ashleigh asked breathlessly when she reached Charlie's side. "When did Mr. Maddock get back? Isn't Jilly here, too?"

"My guess is that Townsend and Maddock are

checking out the yearlings. They got back late last night. Jilly wanted to ride Wonder, but Maddock told her to take the day off—she's been working pretty hard at the track."

"You told her what happened?"

"Yup. She didn't like it, but there wasn't anything she could do."

Ashleigh looked at the track. Jocko was warming up Wonder in the company of several other yearlings. As the riders came around the far turn near where the trainers were standing, they all urged their mounts forward into a fast gallop. For an instant Wonder jumped forward ahead of the others, then as Jocko brought down his whip to urge her to greater speed, she balked. She didn't break from her gallop, but the other horses swept past her, and she made no effort to keep up.

Ashleigh thought she heard Charlie cursing under his breath, and that wasn't surprising. Wonder couldn't have shown Mr. Townsend and Mr. Maddock a worse performance unless she'd stopped dead on the track.

The horses came off the track. Mr. Townsend and the trainers were talking. Ashleigh knew she probably wouldn't like what she heard, but she couldn't stop herself. She moved along the rail in their direction. With all the milling horses in the way, they didn't notice her, but she could hear them clearly.

"What about the filly?" Townsend was asking. "She didn't look like much today."

"She hasn't looked like much at all," Jennings answered. "Her clockings are lousy. She doesn't put anything into it."

"I thought she was coming along pretty nicely before I left," Maddock said.

Jennings shook his head. "She's unpredictable—moody as all get out. She tried to get rid of Jocko a couple of times. He settled her down, but she doesn't want to run."

"You don't think she's a good prospect for two-year-old training in the spring?" Townsend said to Jennings.

"If it were me, I wouldn't waste my time. I can't see the potential."

Ashleigh groaned silently.

"I said I'd give this filly another year," Townsend said. "Her bloodlines are too good to ignore."

"The year's almost up," Maddock reminded him.

"Let me think about it," Townsend said. "But take her out of training. We'll concentrate on the ones who are really showing some promise. Magi looked pretty good—"

Ashleigh turned away and nearly bumped into Charlie. "You heard?" she asked quietly.

"Yup."

"When he says take her out of training, what does that mean exactly?"

"That they'll put her out in the paddock during the day. They'll give the yearlings they want to bring along

*77*

regular cross-country gallops, then start working them back on the track in late winter. They'll be aiming to race them as two-year-olds."

"And they won't be thinking of racing Wonder at all."

"Probably not as a two-year-old—maybe never."

"And if she isn't ever going to race, Mr. Townsend won't keep her on the farm. He'll sell her at auction."

"I can't answer that. Like Townsend said, she's got good bloodlines, but he doesn't usually like to breed untried mares. A mare who doesn't have the heart for racing might pass that on to her foals."

"I'll talk to Mr. Townsend and tell him what happened!" Ashleigh said defiantly.

"I think you'll be wasting your breath. Just like I'd be wasting mine." Suddenly Charlie seemed angry. "I got things to do." He stomped off. Ashleigh stared after him, bewildered. Then she spun around and ran down the drive toward her house. It was all she could do to keep from sobbing.

When she got to the house, she left a note on the kitchen table where her parents would see it: *I've biked over to Linda's.* Then she ran out to the garage, got out her old ten speed, and started pedaling down the drive.

Linda's place was only about a mile up the main road, and Ashleigh had never covered the distance so fast. As she pedaled up the drive she saw Linda leading a horse from the barn toward one of the paddocks. The

March's facilities weren't nearly as big or elegant as Townsend Acres, but everything was immaculately kept.

Linda stared as Ashleigh ran toward her. "What's wrong? You didn't say you were coming over. Just let me put Magpie in the paddock." Ashleigh walked alongside as Linda led the horse to the enclosure and carefully fastened the gate. "Come on up to my room," Linda said.

"I had to talk to you," Ashleigh said when the girls had plopped down on Linda's bed. "Even Charlie doesn't care." Ashleigh blurted out her bad news.

Linda sat quietly listening. "Hmm, I don't know," she said finally.

"What?"

"It may be a dumb idea, but you said Wonder will probably just be put out in the paddock for the winter. What if you asked to exercise her yourself? You know, just on the trails."

"I'm pretty sure Jennings wouldn't like it."

"But if Wonder's out of training, it's not up to him, is it?" There was a scheming gleam in Linda's eye. "Mr. Maddock is the head trainer, and he knows Wonder's history. Ask him."

"You know," Ashleigh said, catching Linda's enthusiasm, "it just might work."

"And with you riding her, you know she'd do better!"

Ashleigh nodded. The thought of approaching Maddock with her request frightened her, but it was for Wonder, she reminded herself, and the worst he could do would be to say no. If he did, she wouldn't be any worse off than she was now.

Ashleigh chose her time carefully. Since Maddock was still working some of the older horses on the track, she waited until all the gallops were over and Maddock had finished checking the horses and talking to their riders and grooms. She saw him coming out of the stable area alone and approached him.

She tried to keep her voice steady, even though she was shaking like a leaf. "Mr. Maddock, there's something I'd like to ask you."

He looked down at her and gave a brief, distracted smile. "If it's quick. I've got a lot to do."

"It's about Wonder . . ." Ashleigh rushed through what she had to say. "I know you'll be taking her out of regular training for the winter. But since I've worked with her all along, would you mind my riding her for exercise once in a while? I wouldn't be alone. Charlie would ride with me, and I know I could handle her."

Ashleigh waited with her heart in her throat.

"Yeah, I've seen you ride Dominator," he said brusquely. "I don't know. . . ." He considered a second longer. "Okay, yeah, what the heck . . . not going to be doing anything with her anyway . . . it can't hurt. Just don't ride her out alone. Might as well keep her fit even if she doesn't go into training. She'll look better at auction."

Relief flooded through Ashleigh. "Thanks, Mr. Maddock! Thanks a lot!" She'd been so sure that he'd say no, she felt like shouting with excitement. Even his mention of auction didn't upset her. At last part of her dream would be coming true—she'd be able to ride Wonder!

She called Linda from the telephone in her parents' office, telling her parents the good news at the same time. Both of them smiled. "I'm surprised he agreed to it," her father said, "but good for you." Then Ashleigh went in search of Charlie and Jilly.

For the first time in weeks, Charlie's blue eyes twinkled. "Just goes to show that you shouldn't give up hope."

"You'll coach us, Charlie, won't you?" Ashleigh asked. "I don't just mean help me with the riding, but train Wonder, too—the way she should be trained."

"You bet I will, missy. I wouldn't pass it up." He chuckled to himself. "It'll be nice to show that Jennings a thing or two."

"You don't think he's already ruined her?"

"Won't know till we get out there . . . but no, I think we've still got a good chance of turning her around."

"Maddock isn't a bad guy," Jilly said. "I know he was all for selling Wonder, and probably still is if she doesn't show any improvement by spring—but he knows his horses, and won't give up on one easily. If we can get her training the way I think she could train by spring, he'll encourage Townsend to keep her."

There was that big *if,* Ashleigh knew. Wonder still might not prove to be a good racehorse, even with all their work. But Ashleigh wasn't going to think about that now. She finally had her chance.

**8**

THE NEXT AFTERNOON ASHLEIGH LED WONDER OUT INTO THE
crisp air. The filly snorted and tossed her head, looking
from side to side. She was nervous, especially when she
saw the saddle Charlie was carrying. She flattened her
ears. Ashleigh spoke soothingly.

"Today's going to be different, Wonder. No one's going to rough handle you. I'm going to ride you, not
Jocko."

Wonder flinched and sidestepped as Charlie laid the
saddle on her back and fastened the girth. "Easy, easy,"
Ashleigh coaxed. But Wonder didn't relax.

"You've got to expect her acting up a little," Charlie
said. "This saddle hasn't brought any good associations
lately. She may be okay when she sees that you're riding her, but be prepared. I'm going to keep the lead line
on her for a while till she quiets down, in case she tries
to bolt."

Ashleigh couldn't believe that Wonder would bolt on her—even after all the filly's horrible experiences in training, but Charlie was right. It was better to be safe than sorry.

Charlie took the lead attached to Wonder's bridle. Ashleigh continued to talk reassuringly to the filly. She slid her foot into the stirrup and swung herself into the saddle. Wonder snorted and backed up with quick, bucking steps, pulling the lead tight in Charlie's hands. Ashleigh gathered the reins as Charlie tried to quiet the filly. "It's okay, girl. It's just me," Ashleigh said softly.

Charlie had already tacked up Dominator and tied him to the paddock rail. He quickly coaxed Wonder in that direction, and still holding Wonder's lead, expertly swung himself into the saddle. The experienced old Thoroughbred stood patiently, eyeing Wonder from time to time.

Wonder stared back with the whites showing around her eyes.

"Let's get her moving," Charlie said tensely. "Just remember, you're on a young, excitable horse who hasn't been treated too good lately. I don't care if you and the filly have been as close as two peas in a pod since she was foaled—she's still young, green, and full of it. Her first instinct if she comes up against something she's not sure of on the trail will be to hightail it and run. You're going to have to be alert every second—ready for anything—with a firm hand on the reins. We're going to have to teach her to forget her bad memories."

Ashleigh nodded, but her concentration was on the fidgeting filly beneath her. Wonder wouldn't settle, and it was taking all of Ashleigh's skill to control her. This wasn't what she'd expected. It made her furious that Wonder should be so frightened. She wished Jennings had never come to the farm!

"Keep a nice balanced seat," Charlie said firmly, scowling as he studied Ashleigh in the saddle. "Heels down, head up. We'll keep her at a walk. I want her nice and relaxed. Get her to start enjoying the ride and stop expecting heavy handling and the sting of a crop. But I don't want her running the show, either. Let her know you're there in the saddle—and if she starts acting up, use your seat, a gentle firm hand, and your voice to get her back on track."

Ashleigh heard his instructions, but she was seriously beginning to wonder if she could carry them out.

They moved side by side up one of the grassy lanes between the paddocks. In the chilly air their breaths misted like smoke. The normally lush grass was browned from frost, and all the trees had lost their leaves. Fortunately there hadn't been a hard freeze yet, so the ground was soft beneath the horses' hooves.

Wonder was ready to spook at the smallest unexpected thing. Ashleigh could feel the filly's tension through the reins.

With Charlie holding the lead rope, they made it to the top of the hill behind the training area, but their progress was far from smooth. Wonder practically toe-danced up the incline, swinging her hindquarters out, arching her neck, and jerking her head.

"Pick up the pace to a trot," Charlie told Ashleigh when they reached a level area overlooking the farm. "I'll keep the lead rope on her. I can see she's not settled."

"She's a bundle of nerves," Ashleigh said through gritted teeth.

"Keep a good grip on those reins—but don't pull on her mouth. Let's see if we can't work some of that nervousness out of her."

When Ashleigh tightened her legs, Wonder jumped forward like a rocket, as if she was trying to jump away from the sting of a whip.

"Hold her!" Charlie barked as Wonder lunged ahead.

Ashleigh hauled on the reins. It took every ounce of strength she had to hold the filly. If Charlie hadn't been holding the lead rope, Ashleigh couldn't have stopped her. She felt the blood draining from her face.

Charlie saw Ashleigh's expression. "She's reacting. She's expecting a whip. Hold her steady."

Even as Charlie spoke, Wonder reacted again. She reared up, struggling to get the bit in her teeth. Ashleigh desperately gripped her mane to keep from falling off.

"Easy, easy," Charlie called to the filly. He pulled Dominator back to a walk, away from Wonder's slashing hooves. "Talk to her," he urged Ashleigh. "Keep talking. Your voice will help."

Ashleigh did, frightened and unprepared for Wonder's behavior. She tried to keep her fear from her voice, but her throat felt tight. "You don't have to be afraid of me. I'm not going to hurt you. You know me, Wonder."

Wonder dropped her forefeet to the ground, but she flung up her head, trying to jerk the reins through Ashleigh's hands. The reins were now slick from the sweat on Wonder's neck. Ashleigh didn't know how much longer she could hold on. Wonder plunged forward again. The force of her momentum nearly pulled the lead from Charlie's hand.

Ashleigh kept talking, hoping her familiar voice might get through.

Slowly—very slowly—Wonder began to listen. She flicked her ears around. Gradually she stopped jerking her head and fighting the reins. Finally she came to a trembling halt.

"That's it," Charlie said almost under his breath. "Keep talking to her. We'll just keep walking her till she works some of this out."

Ashleigh was shaking—trembling as badly as the filly. She could barely keep her hands steady on the reins. If Charlie hadn't been with her, the ride would have ended in disaster. She stared blindly ahead as the shock settled in and only came to her senses again when Charlie spoke urgently.

"Trot her again. It's the only way she's going to learn there's not going to be any whip."

For the barest instant Ashleigh froze, terrified that when she urged Wonder to a trot, the same thing would happen again. She almost cried out, "No, I can't—I'm afraid!" But her pride wouldn't let her. She couldn't look like a loser in front of Charlie.

"Let's trot, Wonder," she said hoarsely, very gently urging the filly forward. She felt Wonder's muscles tense, and almost panicked. Then the filly moved forward, matching strides with Dominator. Ashleigh hardly dared to breathe as they moved on over the grass.

"That's it," Charlie said in a voice meant to soothe both the horse and the girl. "Let's just move along nice and quiet, just a little pleasure ride, nothing more today. We'll trot out a couple of miles and head back—nothing unexpected."

Ashleigh swallowed. She tried to force her muscles to relax, knowing that the filly would feel any tension. She willed her hands to stop shaking and concentrated on getting through the rest of the ride.

As they approached the long, straight lane where the horses were galloped she heard Charlie speaking to her.

"I don't want to do more than that today—too risky

to push her. We're going to have to take it nice and slow. How's she feel now?" he asked.

"Better," Ashleigh said through dry lips. "She doesn't feel like she's going to jump out of her skin."

"Let's head in then—end it on a good note. And make sure you praise her when we get through—let her know she's doing the right thing in calming down."

Ashleigh nodded.

As they walked back through the stable yard, Jilly, who was standing talking with some of the grooms, saw them and started to wave. Then she suddenly frowned and hurried after them, following them back to the paddock.

Ashleigh's legs felt like jelly as she dismounted. She tried to stop her knees from trembling as she pulled up the stirrups. Wonder turned to watch. Her nostrils were flared wide, and only Ashleigh's gentle words and touch helped calm her. "It's not your fault," Ashleigh told the filly. "You're scared. You're afraid of anyone on your back now, aren't you?" Wonder's coat was lathered white with sweat. Was this the way the filly came back from all of her rides with Jocko? A basket case?

The horse whuffed, still on edge, but less jittery now that her saddle was empty. If only Ashleigh felt calmer —but she felt worse.

Jilly hurried up beside them. "What happened?" she asked Charlie and Ashleigh. "You looked white as a ghost when you rode by the stable," she added to Ashleigh.

Ashleigh could only shake her head miserably. Charlie answered, frowning as he removed Dominator's saddle. "The filly's all strung out. It's going to take a lot of time and patience to undo the damage."

Jilly held Wonder as Ashleigh unfastened the girth and lifted the saddle from Wonder's back. "You must have given her some kind of workout," Jilly added, noticing the sweat.

Ashleigh carried the saddle to the paddock rail and rested it on the top. "We only trotted her—or tried to. She's all sweated up because she was so frightened and nervous. I didn't do very well either. I couldn't have handled her by myself. If it hadn't been for Charlie, she would have thrown me or run off."

"I don't know if anyone could have," Charlie said from behind her. "You didn't do bad for a beginner."

His words didn't make Ashleigh feel any better. She'd been so confident and sure of herself when she'd gotten on Wonder's back. Now she felt sick at her lack of skill. Charlie didn't know how scared she'd been—still was.

"You gotta remember what this horse's been through," Charlie said. "Can't expect miracles."

"At this time of year, I could probably find time to ride her the first few days," Jilly offered.

Ashleigh was tempted. The thought of another ride

like the one she'd just had terrified her. Yet it meant so much to her to train Wonder herself—it was part of her dream. If she chickened out now, she'd hate herself someday.

"Might make sense to have Jilly up for a few rides, till she calms down," Charlie said. "But it's up to you."

Ashleigh didn't know what to say. Would Wonder be better off with Jilly, who had loads of experience? Was Ashleigh being selfish in thinking she had to do it herself? She looked at Wonder. The filly was still wild-eyed and breathing heavily. Ashleigh made up her mind. This was her horse, and she had to be the one to undo the damage.

"I've got to do it myself," she said quietly. "I mean, if you think I can, Charlie. If you think my riding her would hurt—if she'd do better with Jilly—"

"Didn't say that, did I?" Charlie answered. "Wonder likes Jilly, but she knows you better. I just don't want you pushing yourself to do something if you don't think you're ready. You had a bad break today—you weren't expecting it. But it's a good lesson, too. Riding a young racehorse isn't as easy as you thought."

Ashleigh sighed. "Yeah, you can say that again."

"Well," Charlie said, "let's get these horses put away before they catch a chill. Take some warm water to wash off the worst of the sweat, missy, then dry her off real good before you put her in her blanket. Maybe some hot bran mash wouldn't hurt."

91

Ashleigh led Wonder inside. She washed her down and dried her, then buckled on her blanket. As she went to make a bran mash, she couldn't stop thinking of their ride—of how little in control of Wonder she'd felt. Would Jilly have been scared, too?

Wonder was calming down now that she was in her stall. She lifted her head from the feed tray and looked over at Ashleigh.

"I expected too much, didn't I?" Ashleigh said. "Everyone was right, and I was wrong. I thought I could make everything go perfectly—just like that!"

Gently Wonder touched Ashleigh's shoulder with her nose. Ashleigh felt her heart melt. "You still love me anyway? Even if you weren't so happy with me riding you. I love you, too, girl. I just hope it's not too late to turn you into a good racehorse."

When Ashleigh went into the house, she called Linda. "Everybody loses confidence sometimes, Ash," Linda said. "Gosh, I do when I try to help my father with training and he yells at me."

"I just thought it would be so different, Linda. You know how Wonder and I are—it's like we understand what each other's thinking—ESP or something. I didn't feel like that today at all. I was scared! I've never been scared on a horse in my whole life, but I thought she'd run away with me."

"There has to be a first time," Linda said. "My father

says that if you're not scared a little, you're heading for a fall."

That night at dinner Ashleigh's parents asked her how her first ride had gone. Ashleigh couldn't bring herself to tell them the truth. "All right," she said vaguely.

They both gave her strange looks. "Only all right?" her mother asked. "Is something wrong?"

"No," Ashleigh said quickly.

Caroline looked up from her plate. "Brad says there's only one way to train—" Suddenly she stopped when she saw the frown on Ashleigh's face.

"I'm not interested in what Brad has to say," Ashleigh snapped.

"Forget it, then," Caro said carelessly.

Fortunately everyone let the subject drop. Ashleigh tried not to think of her fear that night as she got into bed, or the next day while she was in school. She thought of asking Linda to come along to ride Belle, then decided she didn't want Linda to see if she made a mess of the ride again. When Ashleigh got home, she changed into her riding clothes and went to the barn. Her stomach was clenched in a knot of fear.

Charlie greeted her like nothing was wrong. "All set?" he said. He was tacking up Dominator and had Wonder out of her stall, hooked into a set of crossties in the barn. Wonder was already showing signs of unease, swiveling in the crossties, pawing the floor with a front hoof.

Ashleigh did her best to pretend everything was normal—that yesterday had never happened and she was her old confident self. She walked over to Wonder and rubbed Wonder's nose. The horse pulled her head away. Her rear feet danced over the concrete floor. She snorted and refused to stand still.

Wonder grew worse when she saw Charlie approaching from the tack room with the saddle. She whinnied in protest and started backing up in the crossties, until the lines attached to each side of her halter were pulled taut.

"Easy does it," Charlie said as he set the saddle down at the side of the aisle. Ashleigh had taken Wonder's halter and was trying her best to distract the filly.

"It's okay, girl. It's just Charlie and me. You know we'd never hurt you. Come on, Wonder, please. Oh, Charlie, yesterday doesn't seem to have done her any good at all."

"She's got some bad associations to unlearn. Hold it steady, there," he said to Wonder as he slid the saddle with its attached saddle pad onto her back. "Probably should have tacked you up outside. Last time you were tacked up in the barn, you didn't like what happened."

Finally he had the saddle fastened in place, although Wonder didn't help him one bit. "Lead her out," he told Ashleigh.

Ashleigh's hands were shaking as she clipped a lead shank to Wonder's bridle. She unclipped the crossties and quickly led the filly out the barn door. Wonder threw her head up, nearly yanking the shank from Ashleigh's hands. "Please behave, Wonder," Ashleigh pleaded. "What's wrong with you? It's just me. You've never acted like this before."

Wonder was slightly better once they were outside, but she still pulled on the shank, restless and unhappy. Charlie followed them out with Dominator. He mounted the placid older horse and leaned down and took Wonder's lead shank from Ashleigh.

"Why is she acting worse today than yesterday?" Ashleigh asked.

"Don't know. She might be in a mood. Mount up, quick."

Ashleigh panicked. "I can't do it, Charlie. I can't!"

"Yes, you can. Get up there. You gonna quit now when you're just starting? I thought you had some guts."

"I do," Ashleigh whispered.

"Then get up there. Come on, before she gets any more jittery!"

Ashleigh took a deep breath. *This is Wonder,* she reminded herself. *This is the filly I love.* With that in mind, she quickly stepped to Wonder's side, put her foot in the stirrup, gripped the base of Wonder's neck with her left hand, and swung herself up into the saddle. She immediately slid her other foot into the stirrup, settled deep in the saddle, and picked up the reins.

Charlie didn't give Wonder time to react. He instantly started Dominator forward, leading Wonder along. "You're going to do fine, missy," he said as they headed up between the paddock fences. "Just be prepared and forget about yesterday."

Ashleigh looked forward between Wonder's ears. She couldn't relax and was sure that Wonder could sense it. *What's the matter with me?* she thought. *How can I have lost my nerve so completely?*

Charlie kept the horses at a walk for a long time before he said quietly, "Okay, let's try a trot now. Get yourself ready. Sit deep in the saddle, heels down. Take up the reins a little. Be ready for her if she tries to bolt or rear."

Ashleigh did as she was told, talking to Wonder at the same time. "We're going to trot now, girl, but it'll be okay. You don't have anything to worry about." Wonder's ears flicked back, but Ashleigh felt the filly's muscles tremble—just like they had the day before.

Charlie picked up the pace. Ashleigh braced herself, waiting for the explosion. But this time Wonder didn't try to bolt. She broke into a trot, following Dominator's lead.

Ashleigh released her breath in a long, unconscious gasp. So far so good, but she couldn't relax yet.

She concentrated intently as they posted over the

grassy lanes, weaving around the acres of fenced paddocks. She barely noticed the scenery around them. All her thoughts were centered on the filly and her own seat in the saddle. She was amazed to find that they'd circled almost all of the farm and were approaching the long, straight lane leading back to the stable yard.

"I want you to try her without the lead," Charlie said, slowing Dominator to a walk at the top of the lane.

Ashleigh stiffened.

"Nothing to be afraid of. She's been doing fine, and I'll be riding along next to you. We'll ride halfway up the lane, then circle back." Before Ashleigh could protest, Charlie reached over and unsnapped the lead from Wonder's bridle. His movement was so smooth that Wonder didn't even realize what had happened. He settled back in Dominator's saddle. "Okay, let's go. Just nice and easy."

Dominator trotted forward, and almost without any urging from Ashleigh, Wonder trotted after, quickly moving up alongside. Wonder was behaving perfectly. At last, as they circled for the second time, Ashleigh began to relax a little. Maybe it was going to be okay after all.

"Now take her around on your own," Charlie said unexpectedly, pulling Dominator back to a walk. "Keep her going. Nothing to worry about."

Ashleigh didn't have much choice. Wonder seemed

content to keep trotting. But Ashleigh felt a surge of panic. She fought against it. At the point where she and Charlie had turned before, she tightened her left rein. She kept Wonder at an even trot, and started to turn.

The wind suddenly gusted. It lifted some dried leaves from the side of the lane and swept them in a small brown tornado right in Wonder's path. Ashleigh was already looking to her left and didn't even see the leaves until Wonder cried out and suddenly reared up, slashing the air frantically with her front legs.

Ashleigh gasped and made a desperate attempt to catch herself, reaching to grasp Wonder's mane. But she reacted too late. Her feet came out of the stirrups, and she felt herself sliding backward over Wonder's hindquarters. There was nothing to grab, nothing to hold on to. Suddenly she was falling through the air and landing hard on her back with the wind knocked out of her. From the corner of her eye, she saw the flash of one of Wonder's rear hooves. In panic she rolled out of the way, then lay on the grass, gulping for breath.

Charlie was beside her in a second and called down from Dominator's back, "You all right, missy?"

Ashleigh managed to nod, although she wasn't altogether sure yet.

Immediately Charlie shot off after the filly. Wonder was running loose, and in her frightened state was a danger to herself and others. Ashleigh felt stunned and disoriented. She lay on her back for several minutes, realizing just how close she'd come to being kicked. Gradually she was able to breathe more easily, but her lower back was bruised and sore. Slowly, she flexed her legs and arms. Nothing seemed to be broken. She inched up painfully and braced herself with her elbows, then blinked her eyes into focus. She stared down the lane in the direction Wonder had gone, praying Charlie had caught the runaway filly.

What she saw made her face pale, then redden in embarrassment.

Brad Townsend was riding toward her, leading Wonder by her reins! He was staring at Ashleigh where she lay on the grass and was barely hiding his grin. Wincing, Ashleigh forced her back up off the ground, then drew her legs under her and tried to sit. Her pants and jacket were covered with dirt and bits of dead grass and leaves, and her hard hat was twisted at an angle. Ignoring her pain, she pushed herself to her feet. But her legs were far from steady. She wobbled dizzily as she brushed herself off and straightened her hat.

Brad didn't turn Wonder over to Charlie, who was trotting up behind him. He rode right up to Ashleigh before he stopped. From the way Wonder pranced alongside Brad and Townsend Prince, she obviously wasn't hurt, but her eyes were wide and rolling.

"So you couldn't hold her when she spooked, huh?" Brad asked with a smile. He made it sound like Ashleigh was too raw an amateur to control her horse.

Ashleigh seethed and gritted her teeth, but Charlie spoke up quickly in her defense. "Just one of those things. Everyone takes a fall now and again."

"Especially with a filly as unpredictable as this one. Do you really think you can straighten her out and make a racehorse out of her?" He grinned like it was a big joke.

Charlie frowned, but didn't respond. He spoke roughly to Ashleigh. "Well, get back up on her."

Ashleigh's knees felt weak at the thought. Her hands began to tremble. But she couldn't let Brad see her fear —that would be even more humiliating than her fall. Steeling herself and trying to ignore the clenching in her stomach, she took Wonder's reins from Brad and brought them up over Wonder's head. The filly sensed the fear in the air and danced violently sideways. Ashleigh clung to the rein in her hand. "Easy, easy, girl," she said hoarsely.

Charlie reached out and grabbed Wonder's bridle. "Get on up," he said, straining to hold the skitterish horse.

Ashleigh was terrified. Her heart was pounding so hard, she could hear the echo against her eardrums. But Brad was watching. She had to get in the saddle. With her left hand she grasped a handful of mane at the base of Wonder's neck, lifted her left foot and managed to get it into the stirrup. Wonder blew out heavy breaths as Ashleigh sprang up with a push of her right foot and swung her leg over the saddle. She quickly found the other stirrup and gathered the reins, feeling like she was going to choke from the knot rising in her throat.

"Let's go," Charlie said, giving neither Ashleigh nor Wonder time to think. His lips were pressed tightly together in a hard line. With his hand still on Wonder's bridle, he started forward up the lane. Brad had no choice but to move Townsend Prince to the side, out of their way. As they passed him, Ashleigh could tell that he knew exactly how frightened and unsure she felt.

She straightened her back with determination. She had to do this. She had to pretend she had everything under control. When Charlie released Wonder's bridle, she urged Wonder into a trot. The filly was still on edge. "Come on, girl, you can do it," Ashleigh whispered determinedly. "We both can. Don't let him see us looking like jerks!"

Wonder heard the change in Ashleigh's voice—the new resolve. She began to concentrate.

"Good!" Charlie called. "Keep her moving like that and we may get somewhere."

When they turned the horses at the top of the lane, Ashleigh saw that Brad was gone, probably back to the stables. She wondered if he'd stayed long enough to watch any of the good stuff. *Probably not,* she thought angrily.

Thirty minutes later, she and Charlie finished up and rode back through the stable yard. Ashleigh still felt shaky, even though Wonder had behaved like an angel for the rest of the workout. When they came into the yard, a dozen grooms and exercise riders turned and looked their way. Jocko was one of them, and he made a laughing comment that Ashleigh couldn't hear.

"Looks like Brad's passed the word around about your fall," Charlie said.

Ashleigh grimaced and felt her cheeks flush.

"Don't worry about it. Let 'em think that you and the filly are hopeless. They'll stay out of our way and be all the more surprised later. You and I know the horse is starting to make some progress."

Maybe Wonder was making progress, but Ashleigh wasn't so sure about herself.

Then she saw something that made her sit up in the saddle in surprise. "There's my sister talking to Brad." Caro and Brad were standing near one of the stable buildings, deep in conversation.

"That Brad Townsend's not a bad-looking kid," Charlie said.

Ashleigh glared at him. After the way Brad had just acted, how could Charlie say that? And as for Caro, Ashleigh couldn't help feeling that her sister was a traitor.

9

ASHLEIGH WAS EXHAUSTED. IT WAS GOING TO BE ANOTHER LONG, long day. As usual she'd been up early to feed Wonder before school, and she'd had to give a speech in English class that day—a horrifying experience! After school she'd rushed to get her homework done before riding Wonder. And now Charlie was shouting at her.

"Canter her up that rise!" he yelled from Dominator's back. "Don't let the horses in the paddock distract her. Keep her moving!"

Ashleigh tightened her legs and spoke softly to Wonder. "Let's go, girl. You don't want Charlie yelling at you. Show him what you can do." Wonder immediately responded. Her muscles bunched as she struck out with her long legs up the hill. The ground was growing hard from frost, and the cold air stung Ashleigh's eyes. Today Charlie had told her that they would gallop for the first time. She didn't dare think ahead to that.

Little by little over the last week of daily rides, Wonder had improved. The filly was beginning to behave like her old trusting self again. But Ashleigh's self-confidence hadn't completely returned—especially at the thought of a gallop. Ashleigh knew Wonder might still have bad memories of her gallops with Jocko.

At the top of the rise, she glanced back to see Charlie and Linda cantering up behind her.

"Okay, pull her up!" Charlie called.

Ashleigh slowly tightened the reins and leaned her weight back in the saddle. Wonder obediently slowed. "Did I do something wrong?" Ashleigh asked when Charlie and Linda stopped beside her.

"Naw. Looked fine," Charlie said. "I just want to work out a plan." He glanced at Linda. "Feel like taking a gallop on Dominator?"

"Sure!" Linda said without a second's hesitation.

"Good. Belle can't keep up with Wonder, and I don't want to risk these old bones of mine any more than I have to. Better if I can watch anyway. I'm going to go wait at the other end of the lane. When I drop my hand, start cantering them. Four or five strides into the canter," he said to Ashleigh, "give her more leg and rein, lean forward right over her neck—you know, like when you've galloped Dominator. The filly should be happy enough to follow Dominator's lead, but you be alert every second!"

Ashleigh didn't need to be told that. All she could

think of was Wonder bolting, grabbing the bit, tearing off out of control. Ashleigh made herself take a deep breath—she couldn't think about that or she'd be lost before they even started. She looked over at Linda, and Linda smiled her encouragement.

"You all set?" Charlie asked.

"Yup." Linda grinned.

Ashleigh nodded stiffly.

"As you pass me, start slowing them. Then turn and head back to the top of the lane. Got it?"

Charlie trotted Belle far down the lane before pulling the mare up along the fence and turning to face the girls.

Ashleigh's heart was pounding as she waited for Charlie's signal.

"It'll be fine, Ash," Linda said. "And I'll be right here on Dominator."

"Thanks," Ashleigh answered just as Charlie motioned them to start. Ashleigh urged Wonder forward and she broke smoothly into a canter, matching strides with Dominator on her left. Ashleigh counted their strides. Her stomach was knotted by the fourth stride. She glanced quickly at Linda, saw Linda's subtle nod, and heard her say, "Let's go!"

Ashleigh slid her arms forward along Wonder's neck, loosening the reins, and at the same time increased the pressure of her legs on Wonder's sides. The filly leaped forward, then threw up her head, jerking the reins in

Ashleigh's hands. Ashleigh gripped them more tightly. Wonder was pulling nervously to the right, losing momentum. Ashleigh leaned forward over Wonder's neck.

From the corner of her eye, Ashleigh saw Linda and Dominator surge past and draw away. Wonder saw them too. Suddenly Wonder grunted, and before Ashleigh knew what was happening, the filly took off in pursuit. Ashleigh grabbed a handful of mane to steady herself, then tried to relax and go with the rhythm of the horse beneath her. Wonder's powerful muscles stretched. Her hooves pounded in a steady beat on the grass. All Ashleigh could hear was the sound of the hoofbeats and Wonder's deep, regular breaths as the filly fought to make up the distance between herself and Dominator. The older horse was now several lengths ahead, but Ashleigh could feel Wonder's determination to catch him.

Suddenly she wasn't afraid anymore. Nothing mattered but her and Wonder as they flew along like one, with Wonder's mane whipping back into Ashleigh's face. She knew exactly what Wonder was feeling and could sense the filly's overpowering desire to run her heart out and get in front. Ashleigh felt a surge of pure joy. Wonder did have heart—she was overflowing with heart! Jennings and Brad and all the rest of the doubters were wrong!

Ashleigh looked ahead. The gap between Wonder and Dominator was narrowing. She saw Linda glance back, then urge Dominator to go faster by kneading her hands along Dominator's neck. Neither of them carried whips—just the sight of a whip would be enough to spook Wonder. Ashleigh felt the filly shift herself into a higher gear. Her nose drew level with Dominator's flank, then with Linda's leg in the saddle. Then they were head and head. Dominator wasn't ready to give up. The two horses battled, then with another burst of speed, Wonder got her nose in front, then her head. When Ashleigh chanced a quick glance back, she and Wonder were a length ahead, and Wonder was still running at full speed, drawing away.

Ashleigh was so engrossed in the race and Wonder's performance that she had surged well past Charlie before she realized she had to slow down and pull the filly up. If she *could* slow her down. Wonder didn't want to stop! She ignored Ashleigh's commands as Ashleigh sat up in the saddle and drew back on the reins. *Oh, great, here we go,* Ashleigh thought, *galloping right into the stable yard.* That would be disaster—absolute disaster. She hauled harder on the reins and stood up in the stirrups. "Whoa, girl! Slow down!" Finally Wonder listened. Shaking her head in displeasure, she dropped back into a canter. Ashleigh turned her and headed back toward Charlie.

She couldn't believe how far beyond Charlie they'd ridden. He was going to be furious. But he couldn't be too mad—not after the performance Wonder had given.

Linda had already pulled Dominator up. She was staring at Ashleigh and Wonder with wide eyes. When Ashleigh dared to look at Charlie's face, she saw that the old man wasn't scowling. He'd taken off his hat and was pounding it between his hands in excitement.

"My gosh, Ashleigh," Linda gasped. "You kept telling me she was going to be good, but I never thought she'd be this good! Dominator was cranked all the way out—he was roaring—and you went flying by us like it was nothing!"

"She wanted to run, Linda! I didn't have to do a thing. She did it all by herself. She's got heart!"

"I knew it!" Charlie exclaimed, trotting over on Belle. "I knew it! Darn, but it's nice to be right for a change." He replaced his now totally crumpled hat on his head. "They can't tell this old man he doesn't know what he's doing. I only wish I had a stopwatch out. Hey there, Wonder, you're a feisty little lady. And that was a darn good ride, missy. You didn't start out too well. You were tight as a drum—not relaxing—but you did just fine once you forgot to be afraid."

How could he have known so much just by watching her? Ashleigh wondered.

"We'll work that out of you with more practice—a lot more practice. Now that I'm sure what we've got here, I'm going to be working the two of you hard. It's not going to be easy."

"I don't care," Ashleigh said. "Let's do it!"

Ashleigh was so wrapped up in Wonder's training and her own improvement as a rider that she forgot all about Christmas.

"Only two more days till vacation," Linda said as they hurried to the bus after school. "I can't wait!"

Ashleigh stared at her friend. "Oh, my gosh! I haven't even gotten any presents yet! When am I going to get a chance to go shopping?"

"I was wondering if you'd forgotten." Linda grinned. "You hardly know what day of the week it is lately. My mom and I are going to the mall tonight. Why don't you come?"

"Can I? Thanks, Linda."

On Christmas Day the Griffens invited Charlie to have Christmas dinner with them. Ashleigh had asked Jilly, too, when she found out that Jilly wasn't going home to visit her parents.

Ashleigh and Caroline helped their mother in the kitchen and set the table in the dining room with the best china. Their father took Rory out to the barn with him to check the horses to keep the excited eight-year-old out of their way.

The house smelled wonderful—a combination of roasting turkey and pine. Ashleigh felt her stomach rumble in anticipation of dinner. She'd already been out to the barn to deliver a stocking for Wonder filled with horse treats, and had spent a half hour with the filly, giving her a special Christmas grooming.

Charlie and Jilly arrived just as Mrs. Griffen was taking the turkey from the oven. A gust of fresh, cold air swept into the house with them. "Merry Christmas!" Ashleigh said, taking their jackets. "We're just about ready to eat. Come on into the kitchen. I've got to help bring out the food."

Charlie rubbed his hands together, as if relishing the warmth of the house. The rest of the Griffens echoed Ashleigh's Christmas greetings. "Thanks a lot for inviting me," Jilly said with a smile. "Usually I go to my parents' house, but they're up at my sister's in Pennsylvania this year."

"You're more than welcome," Mrs. Griffen said. "Rory, do you think you can manage to carry these potatoes to the dining room?"

Jilly offered to help Caroline and Ashleigh with the rest of the dishes. Mr. Griffen carried in the turkey, and soon they were all seated around the table, filling their plates.

The conversation of course turned to horses. Jilly was enthusiastic about Wonder. Charlie didn't say much, except to answer Ashleigh's parents' questions, but then Charlie wasn't much of a talker. Ashleigh and Jilly more than made up for his silence.

Later, they all went into the living room for dessert and coffee. The tree twinkled with lights and ornaments, and a fire burned cozily in the fireplace. While Charlie leaned back in an easy chair, Rory excitedly showed him and Jilly his gifts.

It was already growing dark outside when Charlie and Jilly left. As Ashleigh and Caroline were helping their parents clean up, Mrs. Griffen said, "You know, Charlie seems a lot happier than he did last year. He doesn't say much, I know, but he doesn't look so depressed. What do you think?" she asked her husband. "Am I just imagining things?"

"No, I noticed the change in him too." He shrugged. "Maybe he's finally adjusting to being retired."

"The way he is now is an improvement?" Caroline exclaimed. "Boy, he must have been a real grouch before!"

"You just never got to know him very well," Ashleigh said. "I think he's happier because he's been helping with Wonder's training. He feels like he's doing something."

"That won't last," Caroline said lightly.

"What do you mean?" Ashleigh asked.

For a second Caroline looked embarrassed. "Oh, nothing. But Brad says they're only letting Charlie help you with Wonder because he hasn't got anything else to do. It'll be different in spring."

"It is only temporary," their father agreed. "Which is a shame. It seems a pity to waste all his knowledge and experience."

"Brad says his father wants younger trainers who can travel around more," Caroline informed them.

Ashleigh swallowed back her irritation. She was getting pretty sick of hearing, "Brad says, Brad says." She looked at her father. "But if Wonder keeps doing as well as she is, maybe Mr. Maddock will let Charlie keep training her."

Caroline quickly turned away from Ashleigh's hopeful expression and started putting dried dishes in the cupboard. Mr. Griffen shook his head. "It would be nice for Charlie, but I doubt it, sweetheart."

## 10

ON NEW YEAR'S DAY WONDER OFFICIALLY TURNED TWO YEARS old, even though her actual birth date wasn't until early May. The official birth date was a reminder to Ashleigh of how little time they had left before two-year-old training began in late February—and how much she and Wonder still had to learn.

Charlie didn't give her any rest, either. They worked until Ashleigh was ready to drop on her feet. For the time being, no one interfered with what Ashleigh and Charlie were doing with the filly, except the weather. Temperatures dropped in early January. The surface of the ground grew rock hard, and nearly every other day light snow fell. Charlie wouldn't chance galloping Wonder, but he was determined she would be worked anyway.

Bundled in parkas, wool hats, scarves, and lined gloves, Ashleigh and Charlie set out every afternoon, trying to get in at least forty-five minutes of exercise before dark. Charlie's plan was to keep Wonder as fit as possible by building up her muscles with long cross-country hikes done at a trot and canter. His eyes were sharp on Ashleigh's seat as well. He quickly barked out corrections to any flaws he saw.

By now Ashleigh had gotten used to his shouting. She still cringed at times, feeling stupid for not doing the right thing without being told, but Charlie's advice was for the best.

On one of the worst days, when icy footing made it too dangerous to ride, Jilly asked Ashleigh if she wanted to go to the tack store in Lexington with her. Ashleigh jumped at the chance. She was feeling restless not being able to ride, and she liked having a chance to talk to Jilly. There was so much the older girl could tell her about racing—and there weren't that many opportunities for them to talk.

Jilly carefully maneuvered her battered pickup over the slippery roads. Beyond the truck windows the acres of tree-lined pasture were sheeted with a light cover of snow. The top surface of the snow had repeatedly melted and frozen into a hard crust, and now it sparkled, rosy-gray ice, in the slanting afternoon sunshine. Only the long-fingered shadows of the leafless trees stood out as a stark contrast. No Thoroughbreds roamed the paddocks now. They could too easily fall and injure themselves. But the scene was still utterly beautiful to Ashleigh. Jilly must have been thinking the same.

"Gorgeous, huh?" she said after a moment.

"Mmm," said Ashleigh. "Though I wouldn't mind if it got just a little bit warmer so that I could start riding again."

"I know how you feel," Jilly agreed. "I'm getting out of shape. I thought for a while that Maddock was going to send me down to Florida to some of the winter races, but I guess he's not going to now. We don't have as many horses running as he thought, and two of my mounts came up lame and had to be rested."

Ashleigh often thought about the excitement in Jilly's life, imagining herself in Jilly's place. "What does it feel like," she asked, "to ride out to the track with all those people watching from the stands? Do you get nervous?"

Jilly laughed. "Oh, I get nervous, all right, but usually by the time I'm actually on the track, all I'm thinking about is my mount and the race ahead. It's a great feeling!"

"Do the guy jockeys give you a hard time?" Ashleigh knew Charlie's feelings about female jocks—and he probably wasn't alone.

"Yeah, sometimes they do." Jilly frowned. "There're a couple of apprentices who are mean. They wouldn't do anything obvious that the stewards could see—like cutting me off, or deliberately bumping me, or poking my mount with their crop. But they do everything they can to box me in and make things tough. Sometimes I think they're more interested in keeping me from winning than winning themselves." Jilly pushed her blond bangs from her eyes. The rest of her long hair was pulled back in a neat braid, as usual. "But a lot of the guys are nice—especially the successful pros. They don't have anything to be jealous about. Their careers are established, and they can always get rides. They tease me, though." Jilly smiled. "One day I'm going to show them just how good I am."

"You know, I've never even been to a racetrack," Ashleigh said.

"You haven't?" For an instant Jilly turned and gaped, then quickly looked back at the road. "I don't believe it. Living on a racing farm—"

"We didn't always. The farm we had before was strictly breeding. My parents didn't have any reason to go to the track."

"You'll have to come with me sometime then! Maybe this spring when Keeneland opens. You could come on a weekend and stay in my room."

Ashleigh's face lit up. "I'd love to."

"You'll love everything about the track! I even like the rotten stuff—mucking out stalls once in a while, sitting around twiddling my thumbs while the male apprentices are getting rides and I'm not. You can always feel a kind of excitement in the air."

They had reached the outskirts of Lexington. The rolling paddocks had been replaced by more and more housing developments, and traffic was heavier. Jilly turned confidently down several side roads. Within minutes she pulled up in front of a huge tack store and swung the truck into an empty parking space.

"Been here before?" she asked Ashleigh.

"No." Ashleigh sized up the store. "Only to the store in the mall."

"This one's the best around. They've got *everything*. Maddock asked me to pick up a few girths and some saddle pads, but I want to look around, too. They're always getting new stuff."

They climbed out of the truck and went through the swinging doors of the store into a huge, high-ceilinged room. The first scent that hit Ashleigh's nose was leather. And it was everywhere—saddles, bridles, boots, gloves. Ashleigh didn't know where to look first. This was a horse lover's heaven.

Jilly knew exactly where she was going and led Ashleigh toward the back. They passed a clothing department, then a footwear department. Another department was devoted to headgear; another to horse blankets, sheets, and leg wraps. Jilly stopped in the saddlery section. While she talked to the clerk, Ashleigh roamed up and down the aisles, looking at the softly gleaming saddles.

She'd never seen so many different kinds of saddles

in her life. They even had beautifully tooled Western saddles, which Ashleigh hadn't expected. She saw an all-around English riding saddle that would be great for cross-country rides. Farther down she found a feather-light, hand-crafted racing saddle. She imagined how perfect it would be for Wonder. She lovingly fingered it, then looked at the price and gasped.

Jilly walked up behind her. "Nice, huh? That's the one I like too." Jilly gently rubbed her hand over the rich brown leather. "If I could afford it. Mr. Townsend has a few handmade saddles, but Maddock keeps them for his best horses." Jilly pointed to another saddle. "This is like the one you're using for training."

The second saddle was very similar—light, with no unnecessary parts—but much more rudely crafted. It was like comparing a costume jewelry bracelet with the twenty-four-karat-gold article displayed in a jeweler's window.

For the next hour the girls avidly examined boots, crops, hard hats. Ashleigh drooled over a pair of fawn-colored riding breeches and an incredibly warm but lightweight down vest that would be perfect for her excursions with Charlie on cold winter days. She saw a half dozen other things she longed to have, too. She'd outgrown most of the riding clothes her parents had given her the year before. The bottoms of her good riding breeches were way up above her ankles, and lately she'd been going out in jeans. But the things she picked out were always so expensive.

"Look at these gloves." Jilly sighed. "I wasn't going to buy anything, but they're so pliable. I'd be able to keep my hands warm and still feel everything in the reins. What do you think?"

"They're nice," Ashleigh said appreciatively, fingering the leather.

"It'll take most of the extra money I've saved, but I'm going to get them." Jilly grinned and walked over to the cashier.

The girths and saddle pads Jilly had picked up for Maddock were already packed in the bed of the pickup. The girls climbed in the cab and started back to Townsend Acres.

"Thanks for bringing me along," Ashleigh said as they wove through traffic.

"Anytime. And I mean it about coming to the track with me this spring."

"Great!" Ashleigh hoped Jilly wouldn't forget her promise by then.

It was five o'clock and nearly dark when they got back to the farm. First they unloaded Maddock's supplies, then walked down the drive toward the yearling barn to visit Wonder.

Charlie was outside, pacing. "Where you two been?"

he said without preamble. "I saw the truck come up the drive."

"Shopping in Lexington." Ashleigh smiled.

"At the tack store," Jilly explained. "I had to get some stuff for Maddock."

"Should have told me." Charlie slapped his hands against his arms. "Cold out here. I had an idea about what you could be doing as long as this rotten weather holds out," he said to Ashleigh. Without another word he went inside, and Ashleigh and Jilly followed.

"Here, I've already got it set up." Charlie dragged a bale of hay out into the middle of the aisle near Wonder's stall. He had already put a racing saddle over it. "This'll give you practice with your seat," he explained. "You sit in a jockey's crouch. Then you balance yourself, moving your weight back and forth just like you would on Wonder's back. Go ahead. Try it."

Ashleigh looked uncertainly at the bale of hay, but followed Charlie's instructions. He and Jilly stood beside her. Charlie was right. As Ashleigh balanced over the bale, she could feel her riding muscles working.

"This is good," she said.

Unfortunately, Wonder only saw the hay as food. She leaned her head way out over her stall door, watching. Then she grabbed a mouthful of hay and tore it from the bale.

"Hey!" Ashleigh laughed. "Stop eating my horse. You've got hay in your hay net."

Wonder responded by shaking her head, lipping up another mouthful, and tearing it away. Ashleigh jumped off, slid the bale farther into the center of the aisle, and got a disgruntled look from Wonder.

"I shouldn't have put temptation in her way," Charlie said.

"Wait a minute." Jilly snapped her fingers. "I've got a great idea. Something I used to do." She shot off in the direction of the tack room and returned seconds later with an old broom and a bridle. She fastened the bridle around the head of the broom, then stuck the pole into the end of the bale.

"This will help give you a better feel of the positioning of your arms," she told Ashleigh. "You'll use the same motion you use when the filly stretches her neck forward and back at a gallop. See, like this." She positioned herself in a jockey's crouch and picked up the reins and held them as she would while galloping, with her elbows bent and her forearms and hands in a straight line. She leaned forward from the waist, moving her arms and hands forward at the same time. Then she leaned back.

Charlie nodded in agreement. "Go ahead, try," he said to Ashleigh.

Ashleigh climbed back on and did as Jilly had demonstrated. It wasn't anything like sitting on a moving horse, but she could feel the muscles in her arms and shoulders working.

121

"Too bad we can't mechanize this contraption," Charlie said.

"Somebody already has," Jilly told him with a grin. "A New York jockey, using a barrel instead of a bale of hay. But it'll cost you."

The weather stayed miserable, and Ashleigh was getting anxious. She knew regular training would start in another month. She and Wonder had to be ready—but they wouldn't be ready unless they put in more practice on Wonder's gallops. All they could do when they did go out was practice at a slower pace.

By late January Charlie was getting to be a real bear. He was having Ashleigh practice breaking Wonder into a gallop from a dead stop. Ashleigh was sure she was doing everything exactly right, urging Wonder forward with her legs and hands at Charlie's signal. But Wonder jumped out lazily, dancing sideways before finally breaking into a gallop.

Charlie immediately stopped her. "What are you doing?" he yelled angrily. "You think you're ever going to be a good rider throwing away your reins like that? Do it again! And this time let her know you're in the saddle!"

"But I never had any trouble with Dominator, and you said not to be too hard with the reins."

"Dominator's a well-trained horse. This filly isn't," Charlie barked back. "And there's a happy medium with the reins. You have to feel a little tension in them so you know you're communicating. You don't want them so tight you jerk on her mouth—but you don't want them hanging loose in your hands like a couple of useless ribbons. The filly didn't know what you wanted her to do. Go on—back to the line!"

On days like this Ashleigh wondered if she'd ever be as good a rider as she wanted. Would she ever get it all together in one piece—the legs, the reins, the seat? It didn't make her feel any better to see a couple of exercise riders trot past as Charlie had her start again and again. He totally ignored the riders. He was intent on the lesson, but Ashleigh felt their eyes, and because of it did worse than she had the first time. And by now, Wonder was getting restless and picking up on Ashleigh's frustration and confusion.

Finally Charlie got off Belle and strode over. "Get off. I'll have to show you. Can't call it quits on a bad note with the horse not knowing what's right and wrong."

Feeling close to tears, Ashleigh dismounted, took Belle's reins from Charlie, and led her to the side as Charlie swung into Wonder's saddle.

"Now watch," Charlie said from the starting line. "You see the tension I've got on the reins. You see they're still in a straight line along her neck, from her mouth back to my hands. You see there's no loop in them."

Ashleigh nodded mutely.

Charlie turned his attention to Wonder. "All right. Now we're going to do a nice smooth start. One, two, three—"

On three, Charlie had Wonder leaping off the line in a dead-straight gallop. Ashleigh stared at his every movement, trying to see what he was doing, but he made it seem so effortless. He let Wonder gallop a short way up the lane, then slowed and turned her. He trotted back.

"See what I mean?" he said.

Ashleigh swallowed, not sure she'd seen anything at all. "I guess."

"That's it for today. The filly's had enough. Remember what I showed you for tomorrow. You're going to get it right then."

That night after dinner, all Ashleigh wanted to do was soak in a hot bath.

Caro came into the bedroom as Ashleigh was gathering up her pajamas and robe to take into the bath. She took one look at Ashleigh's face and shook her head.

"Do you really think it's worth it?" she asked.

"What?" Ashleigh said tiredly.

"All this riding and practicing on Wonder."

Ashleigh frowned. "Of course it is! Why do you say that?"

Caro was silent for a second, then seemed to make up her mind. "Well, I wasn't going to say anything about it, but Brad says you and Charlie are wasting your time.

He doesn't think Wonder will ever turn into anything or go back into training."

"What does Brad know?" Ashleigh shot back angrily. "I guess he told you I fell, and that he brought back Wonder when she ran off! But he hasn't even seen us since then. Wonder's doing great now—after we undid the damage Jennings and Jocko did!"

Caroline looked down and twisted her pinky ring. "Ashleigh, when I was up at the stables today, a couple of the exercise riders told me that . . . that you're not an experienced enough rider." She finished the last in a rush, took a quick breath, and plunged on. "They said you and Charlie baby Wonder—that if she looks like she's improving, it's only because you don't ask much of her. They don't think she'll make it if she runs with other horses."

"Well, they're wrong!" Ashleigh cried. She'd clenched her fists so hard, her nails were biting into her palms. "Who were you talking to? Jocko?" she demanded.

"No, two of the other riders. Jocko wasn't around. Ash, I'm only telling you because I don't want you to be—"

Ashleigh cut her short. "Funny nobody tells *me* that!"

"They're afraid to. They don't want to hurt your feelings."

"But it's okay to talk behind my back! I suppose Brad thought I was lousy too."

"Well . . . I was talking to him when the riders came over," Caroline admitted.

"And he agreed with them. What are you hoping he'll do—ask you out or something? Fat chance. Mr. Know-It-All isn't going to have anything to do with the breeding managers' daughter," Ashleigh taunted.

"As a matter of fact, we've already been out a couple of times, and we're going to the movies together tonight. He's picking me up at six-thirty."

Ashleigh gaped at her sister. She couldn't believe it. Caroline had been going out with Brad? "You traitor!" Ashleigh choked. "You're taking Brad's side. You'd believe anything he said just to get a date with him. You *hope* Wonder and I will do lousy. That way Brad'll look so smart, won't he?"

"I'm not taking Brad's side!" Caro shouted back.

"Oh, no? First he tells you how rotten Wonder is, then you tell me I'm a crummy rider because Brad says so—and now you're going out with him!" Ashleigh screeched, close to tears.

"I'm going out with him because I want to! I like him."

"You care more about Brad Townsend than you do your own sister!" Ashleigh didn't wait for Caroline's answer. She flung her pajamas and robe in her sister's face, spun on her heel, and raced from the bedroom as the tears broke loose and cascaded down her cheeks. Rory came running down the hall from his room, and

Ashleigh nearly collided with him as she rushed for the stairs.

"What's wrong?" he cried. "Why were you and Caro shouting? Why are you crying?"

Ashleigh could only shake her head. As she pounded down the stairs, her parents came into the hall from the living room.

"What's going on?" Her father scowled. "What were you and Caro screaming about?"

"Ask *her*!" Ashleigh gasped, grabbing her jacket from the coatrack and rushing out the door.

"Just a minute, young lady—" her father began. But Ashleigh was already gone, running up the drive to the barn. She heard the door open and close behind her, but kept running. Only when she reached the security of Wonder's stall did she stop. She threw herself against the stall door and sobbed. Wonder, nickering, leaned her head over the door and nuzzled Ashleigh's hair. Ashleigh reached up and held the filly's head close to her own. Wonder stood patiently, blowing out soft, sweet-scented breaths as Ashleigh sobbed. "I hate her," Ashleigh choked. "Oh, Wonder, I feel so awful—"

Ashleigh felt a gentle hand on her shoulder and heard her mother's voice. "Whatever happened must have been pretty terrible. Tell me," she said quietly.

In a shaking voice Ashleigh slowly repeated what Caroline had said. Her mother immediately drew Ashleigh close. "I can see why you're upset. But I'm sure she didn't mean it the way it sounded."

"Yes, she did." Ashleigh gulped back another sob. "She believes it, too. She really thinks Wonder and I are lousy. Why did she even tell me?"

"Maybe she thought that you'd be less hurt hearing it from her than hearing talk in the stables."

"All this time the other riders have been talking about me behind my back. I didn't even know."

"Not everyone. Caroline only talked to two of them. And some of their comments might have been made out of jealousy, you know."

"No. They're probably right. I'm *not* good enough! I couldn't even handle Wonder the first couple of times I rode her. And Charlie got mad at me today!"

"But you're getting better, aren't you? I'm sure Charlie would tell you if he didn't think you were up to snuff. He'd tell you that you were wasting your time. Maybe he loses his temper once in a while, but he must think you've got talent. Sweetheart, everyone's bound to hear things said about them that are hurtful. Just keep believing in yourself."

"But how could Caro be such a traitor and go out with Brad? And after he said rotten stuff about me?"

"So that's the rest of the problem." Mrs. Griffen sighed. "Ashleigh, I really don't think Caroline sees going out with Brad as taking sides. Remember, Caro's not a horsewoman. She doesn't understand your devotion to Wonder and why it's so vitally important to you that Wonder does well. She'd never feel that kind of tie with a horse. Other things are important to her. You and I are more alike. I know how you feel about Wonder—if I didn't, I wouldn't be spending my life working with horses. But it's more than just Wonder, isn't it? You need to prove *you* can do it, too."

"Yes . . ." Ashleigh looked at her mother.

"You will—if I know you and this filly. Just don't let the opinions of others get in your way."

Wonder blew another soft breath on Ashleigh's cheek. She gazed down at Ashleigh, and Ashleigh sighed and gave a watery smile.

"I think she's trying to tell you something," Mrs. Griffen said. "She believes in you."

Ashleigh gently kissed Wonder's velvety nose. "Okay, girl. I won't give up yet."

**11**

ASHLEIGH FOUND IT HARD TO LOOK AT THE OTHER EXERCISE RID-
ers without wondering which of them had been talking
about her. It still made her furious to think of it, and to
know that Caroline was dating Brad—the biggest critic
of them all. When she told Charlie about the gossip the
next afternoon, he gruffly told her that he'd already
heard the same comments and to ignore them. "So we
give them a big surprise come spring when we take this
filly out on the track and show them what she can do."

"Do you think it would be better for Wonder if Jilly
rode her?" Ashleigh couldn't stop the question. It had
been nagging at her.

"Nope, I don't," Charlie said. He wouldn't say any
more.

Linda had the same advice as Charlie. "Look, Ash,"
she said, "I saw her run. She's going to be good. And
*you're* going to be good. Don't listen to anyone else."

But Ashleigh had been watching the horses that Maddock had chosen to go into two-year-old training. They looked good too. Deep inside she knew that she and Wonder weren't up to their level yet. Wonder had fallen too far behind in early training. But she *had* to be as good as the other two-year-olds, or she'd never go on to race.

Charlie's growing irritability didn't help either. "Darn cold," he grumbled, "enough to make you want to move south. Let's just hope it breaks soon. We need to get in some decent gallops, and I want to start clocking her."

"Charlie's turned into a real grouch!" Ashleigh complained to Linda as they went into homeroom a few mornings later. "I can't stand it. He's always frowning, and he's starting to make Wonder nervous too."

"He's probably just getting bored. My father always gets grouchy when the weather's bad and he can't train. But I heard it's supposed to get warmer this weekend."

"Boy, I hope so!" Ashleigh sighed as they walked to their seats. The bell hadn't rung, and most of the kids were standing around talking. Corey saw them and hurried over, looking like she had some hot gossip to pass on.

"Hey," she said to Ashleigh. "I didn't know your sister was going out with Brad Townsend! Why didn't you tell me?"

Ashleigh scowled. She wasn't quite as angry with

Caroline since Caroline had apologized, but it still totally annoyed her that Caro was going out with Brad and walking around in a dreamy daze because of it. "You know Brad?" she asked evasively.

"Not to talk to, but everybody who's into horses at all knows who the Townsends are. So when did she start going out with him?" Corey asked eagerly. "I saw them at the movies last night, and Jennifer said someone had seen them at the concert at Rupp."

"Oh, a month ago, I guess."

"You're kidding!" Corey yelped. "Oh, wow! I can't wait to tell Jennifer."

Ashleigh groaned under her breath.

"But I thought your sister didn't like horses," Corey added, puzzled.

"She doesn't much." The bell rang, saving Ashleigh from more questions. She threw Linda a relieved look as Corey rushed for her seat.

That weekend the weather did break. The sun shone and the temperature climbed to forty-five. "A heat wave," Ashleigh said to Linda on the phone Saturday morning. "I know Charlie will want to go out. Can you come over for a ride?"

"Sure," Linda said. "I'll be right there—even if it is going to be a muddy mess."

Linda was right about the mud. By late morning the ground was gluey. As Ashleigh, Linda, and Charlie rode out, the horses' hooves sank deeply into the glop and made sucking noises as they lifted their feet.

The mud didn't seem to bother Charlie at all. He wasn't actually smiling, but he was pretty close to it. "Have to get her used to all kinds of conditions," he said cheerfully. "She's bound to be running on some sloppy tracks."

Ashleigh nodded as she wiped a glob of mud, kicked up by Dominator's hooves, from her cheek.

"We'll do some gallops today. Don't imagine we'll get very good times, but she needs the practice."

When they reached the lane after trotting the horses over the trails to warm them up, Charlie gave the two girls instructions. "I'm going to clock her—just to get an idea of how she goes on a bad surface. We'll gallop them two furlongs—a quarter mile. I've already marked it out on the fence along here. But if she doesn't like the surface," Charlie said to Ashleigh, "don't push her too hard. Let's just see how it goes."

As Charlie rode Belle up to the quarter-mile mark, Ashleigh turned to Linda. Linda looked calm and relaxed, but Ashleigh felt a twinge of fear at the thought of racing over such a slippery surface. Either of the horses could lose its footing and fall. "Have you ever galloped in the mud—for training, I mean?" Ashleigh asked.

"A couple of times," Linda said, "but on my dad's

track. It's going to be messy. We're going to need these goggles."

"Whew, thanks for reminding me." Ashleigh reached up, pulled the plastic goggles down from above the brim of her helmet, and adjusted them comfortably over her eyes. Charlie had planned ahead that morning and brought both Ashleigh and Linda a pair.

Ashleigh had barely gotten herself settled when Charlie's hand fell. Linda was ready, and Dominator shot off. But Ashleigh had lost valuable seconds. She put her fears aside and heeled Wonder forward. The filly jumped out in pursuit. Mud flew back from Dominator's hooves. Ashleigh could barely see, but she could feel Wonder gathering speed rapidly. The horse wasn't letting the flying mud stop her. Her strides lengthened, even though she had to work harder to get traction on the slippery surface. The mud coated Ashleigh's goggles. Dominator was still in the lead. Ashleigh tried to gauge the distance between them, but the coating of mud made it impossible. She had to trust Wonder to get them in front—she had no other choice.

"Go to it, girl!" she cried over the sound of pounding hooves. "Let's get 'em!"

At her words, Wonder dug in. She stretched her neck, and Ashleigh leaned into Wonder's flying mane. Ashleigh knew they must be pulling astride of Dominator because the mud wasn't coming back at her so heavily. She let Wonder run. She could hear Dominator's pounding hooves and huffing breaths beside her. She rubbed her head quickly against her sleeve, clearing a section of her goggles. She could see Dominator's dark head now to her left. Then, with another burst of speed, Wonder surged past the other horse, pounding on without any urging from Ashleigh.

From the corner of her eye, Ashleigh saw the dark blur of Charlie and Belle as she and Wonder pounded past. Only then did she take full control of the filly again, tightening the reins and lifting her weight away from Wonder's neck.

"Okay, girl, whoa. Slow it down . . . slow it down." Wonder responded obediently. "Good girl," Ashleigh said. "Good girl."

She brought the filly down to a canter and circled her back, then pushed the goggles up on her forehead so she could see. Linda rode up next to her. Linda had pushed her goggles up too. Ashleigh glanced at her and started to giggle. "You look like a raccoon in reverse."

"So do you." Linda laughed.

"Wonder and Dominator don't look much better." Wonder's coppery coat was now a dull shade of pale brown, but Wonder didn't seem to mind. The filly pranced, tossing her head. "You know you did a good job, don't you?" Ashleigh teased. "You're just too smart."

Charlie trotted up, waving his stopwatch. "You have

any idea what kind of time you did?" he called. "The quarter in twenty-three—in the mud!"

"Is that good?" Ashleigh worried. She couldn't tell from Charlie's expression whether he was pleased or not.

"Good?" he cried. "I'd have been glad for twenty-five. It's incredible! And if she can do that in this slop, I can't wait to see what she can do on a fast surface. How'd she feel?" he rushed on. "Tired at all? She feel like she'd used herself up—or did she have more left?"

"She didn't feel tired at all! She would have kept going if I'd let her." Ashleigh could feel the drying mud crack on her cheeks as she grinned. "So you're happy, Charlie?"

"Happy? You just made this old man's day. We got something here, missy. We sure do."

"Wait till the rest of them hear her times!" Linda exclaimed. "That'll change their minds about Wonder and you, Ash!"

"Don't start telling anyone yet," Charlie said. "Let's keep this between us for the while."

Ashleigh stared at him. "How come?" She'd been waiting for the chance to tell Wonder's critics—especially Caro and Brad—that they were dead wrong!

"I've got my reasons," Charlie answered. "And I want to do some more clockings. Too easy for people to say that one good clocking was a fluke. Just bide your time, missy. We've got a few weeks yet before training starts, and before that we've got some more work to do."

Ashleigh swallowed her disappointment. It was hard to be patient when she'd waited so long for this moment. But Charlie was right. Linda gave her a smile. "At least *we* know what she can do!" she said.

"Yeah!" Ashleigh rubbed a loving hand over Wonder's muddy neck. "You're going to be something special!"

They walked the horses back through the stable yard. With the break in the cold weather there was more activity around the barns, though none of the other horses had been taken out on the trails that afternoon. Ashleigh glanced over as faces turned to watch them pass.

"So you haven't given up yet?" a teasing voice called. "Must be pretty desperate to go out in this."

Ashleigh glared in the direction of the voice, then remembered what Charlie had said and changed her frown to a secret smile. Charlie didn't seem to have heard the comment. "Twenty-three in the mud," he kept saying gleefully under his breath.

Linda and Ashleigh exchanged a wink.

They'd just dismounted and started untacking the horses when Caroline and Brad walked over from the stable area.

"Oh, God, look at you!" Caroline exclaimed when

she got a good look at Ashleigh. "You didn't fall, did you?"

"No, I *didn't*," Ashleigh said sharply, all too aware that Brad was giving her and Wonder a scrutinizing look. He didn't look the least bit impressed. Ashleigh had the urge to say something about Wonder's time and wipe the look off his face, but she bit back her words. Instead she said lazily, "You didn't take Townsend Prince out today, Brad?"

"No. He's doing so well he can afford to miss a few days of workouts."

His tone clearly implied that Wonder and Ashleigh couldn't afford any time off. Ashleigh turned her back on him as she lifted Wonder's saddle.

"She starting to behave herself any better?" Brad asked with a grin.

"Yep—with the right kind of handling."

"But you haven't had her on the track yet, have you? Sure she's not going to drop back into the pack like she did before?"

Charlie cut in before Ashleigh could answer. "She's doing just fine. She's just where I want her."

Ashleigh looked around in time to see Brad lift his eyebrows skeptically. Then he motioned to Caroline, and the two of them walked on down the barn toward Townsend Prince's stall. Brad's careless voice drifted back to Ashleigh. ". . . You know Dad and Maddock are only letting them work the filly because they feel sorry for them . . . hopeless cause. . . ."

Ashleigh froze. She started to spin on her heel, but suddenly felt a hand on her arm.

"It's only talk," Charlie said, "and it won't do you a bit of good to get upset."

"But he's talking about us!"

"I've heard worse. Besides, whether they feel sorry for us or not, we've got our chance with the filly. That's all that matters."

If Brad's comments did anything, they made Ashleigh and Charlie work that much harder. They were improving with each workout, and the weather was improving too. When Linda couldn't come to Townsend Acres, Jilly rode Dominator. She was just as determined to see Wonder do well. "I want to see Jocko's face when this little lady finally gets back to the training ring. I haven't said anything to him, but he knows I've been out riding with you guys, and he's always got some nasty comment to make. It'd never occur to him that it was his riding that made the filly go wrong."

"I've been thinking," Ashleigh said, chewing her lip. "What if they don't let me ride Wonder?" It was a thought Ashleigh had tried to avoid, but the time was growing near when she'd have to face it.

Both Charlie and Jilly were silent for a moment. "Let's not start worrying yet," Charlie finally said.

"But we have to!" Ashleigh cried.

"I'll ride her," Jilly said. "She knows me, and you and I ride alike."

"What if you're not here? If you're away at the track or something?"

No one had an answer to that.

"Let's gallop 'em," Charlie said, quickly changing the subject.

Ashleigh spent that night in her room, reading. She had a book report due in a couple of days, and she'd been spending so much time riding that she'd gotten behind. The phone rang about eight-thirty, and Caroline came tearing in from the bath with a towel wrapped around her to answer it. Ashleigh had a pretty good idea who that might be. It was confirmed when she heard Caro coo, "Oh, hi, Brad. I was hoping you'd call. How was the auction?"

Caro curled up on her bed with a blissful expression while she listened. "So your father bought a two-year-old. He's going to let you train it? Great! Yeah, I know. Aside from Townsend Prince, you've only got a couple here that look promising. . . ."

Ashleigh slammed her book shut in disgust. Caro's soppy sweetness was bad enough, but to hear her talking about horses and training like she was some kind of expert was more than Ashleigh could take.

She jumped off her bed and headed for the door. She'd read in the den.

* * *

Wonder's times remained good, and Charlie stretched out the distance of the gallops, but without using the regular training oval they were limited.

"I've got to get her out on that oval," Charlie grumbled to the girls. They had gathered in Jilly's small room one rainy afternoon in late February.

"Can't you just tell Maddock you're going to use the track?" Jilly said.

"We're not supposed to be doing heavy training with her, remember? And I don't want the whole stable yard knowing what we're doing. I want to get her used to the track again when it's nice and quiet—no other distractions."

Jilly sat up straighter. "I just thought of something! There's a trainer's conference next weekend in Lexington."

"So?" Ashleigh said.

But Charlie understood. "Jennings and Maddock will be gone."

"And some of the riders."

Ashleigh and Charlie both started to smile. "We could take her out late—when the rest of them are all in for dinner," Charlie planned. "I don't care so much if they see us jogging her around, but I don't want anyone getting curious yet about her times."

"Why?" Linda asked.

"Because if she looks too good, someone just might

decide to take the training out of our hands. And then where would the filly be? You know what'll happen if anyone starts handling her too rough again."

"But aren't you afraid that will happen anyway, once we let the other trainers see her stuff?" Ashleigh asked.

"We'll have her far enough along that they'll see the finished product and won't be tempted to undo the good training she's had. I'll have a word with Maddock then, but not before."

"Do you think anyone will get mad that we're using the track when the trainers aren't around?"

"Let me worry about that," Charlie said. "When are they all heading out?" he asked Jilly.

"Friday afternoon."

"Then we'll plan on working her Friday night."

"It'll be dark," Ashleigh said.

"Of course," Charlie said roughly. "But there'll be enough light from the stable yard. If you're expecting it to get easy on us anytime soon, we might as well give up now."

"Oh, no," Ashleigh said quickly. "I'll be there!"

"ALL SET?" CHARLIE SAID TO ASHLEIGH AND JILLY.

Ashleigh double-checked Wonder's girth, then led the filly out of the barn into the darkness. Jilly and Dominator followed. Linda hurried up beside Ashleigh. Charlie walked in the lead. The lights along the drive cast enough brightness that they could easily see their way up toward the training oval. But instead of following the drive past the stable yard, Charlie headed them off across the grass under the trees.

"Less likely to see us this way," Charlie said.

"I feel like a spy, sneaking around." Linda giggled. "This is fun."

"Not if someone catches us and kicks up a stink," Ashleigh said, but she was grinning with excitement too. "Had all the staff gone in to eat when you came down?" she asked Jilly.

"Yup, and they were mostly grooms. All the riders

except Tony Black and Bob Niles went to Lexington, and they're good friends with Charlie. They wouldn't say anything if they saw us."

Still, Ashleigh felt a little tingle go down her spine at the thought of being caught. It made the night's ride seem like a real adventure.

"Shhh," Charlie whispered. "Enough jabbering." He motioned them to a stop in the shadow of the trees, although the leafless branches didn't offer much protection. "I don't want to raise my voice out on the track, so here's what we're going to do. Jog them around once to warm them up. The two of you stay together. One of the things we've got to do tonight is get Wonder used to running close into the turns again. Jilly, you take Dominator to the outside so she isn't tempted to run out. Then I want you to slow-gallop them head and head for another mile. This is a mile track. You've got four turns to bend her around, so keep that in mind. The last half mile, let 'em out all the way. I'll be clocking them, so be ready to get down to business when you come around the turn. Got it?"

"I hope so," Ashleigh said nervously. "I've never ridden on the track before."

"Watch Jilly. This isn't a race. She'll give you the signal when to start galloping and breezing. And keep an eye out when you're jogging around. Get familiar with the track."

Charlie strode off. He and Linda stopped by the track entrance as Ashleigh and Jilly rode on.

"Good luck," Linda called softly.

"There's nothing to be nervous about," Jilly added in the same quiet tone.

Ashleigh wasn't so sure. Wonder snorted and tossed her head, not used to training in the dark, and she seemed to be remembering her last experience on the track. She was uneasy and distracted. Instead of listening to Ashleigh, she turned her head from side to side, looking at everything around her and obviously not liking what she saw.

"Get her moving, and she should settle down," Jilly said. Jilly moved Dominator to the center of the track and motioned for Ashleigh to take Wonder inside, closer to the rail. "Let's go," Jilly whispered, urging Dominator into a trot.

Ashleigh had to work to get the filly going. Wonder tried to move out, away from the rail. Ashleigh tightened her left rein, and Jilly kept Dominator close beside them on the right, leaving Wonder no alternative but to trot forward. But Wonder wasn't happy. She tossed her head and skittered her hindquarters around, telling Ashleigh through every signal the filly knew that she wanted no part of the track.

Ashleigh didn't give in. She held her legs tight on Wonder's sides and gripped the reins firmly. "There's nothing to be afraid of, Wonder."

Wonder's ears flicked back for an instant, then she snorted nervously and threw up her head, fighting Ashleigh's commands. Ashleigh could feel the sweat breaking out on Wonder's neck—just like it had the first time Ashleigh had ridden her. Ashleigh remembered that horrible day too well!

They came unevenly around the turn and down the darker backstretch. Wonder was like a coiled spring waiting to snap. Ashleigh felt her own panic growing—but she forced it down. She glanced over at Jilly, riding so close beside her.

"Nice and easy," Jilly said. "You're doing fine."

"She doesn't like it."

"Give her time. Let's open them up—canter, then slow gallop. She can work it out of her system."

Ashleigh wanted to cry, "No!" but it was too late. Jilly had already put Dominator into a canter. Ashleigh knew Wonder was going to explode out of control—rear up or buck her out of the saddle. Wonder trembled beneath her. And Wonder did explode, straight into a frenzied gallop. Ashleigh clutched at the reins, grabbed a handful of mane, and tried to balance herself. At least she had been prepared and hadn't lost control of the filly.

She hauled back on the reins, trying to slow Wonder's headlong flight. "Easy—easy, girl!" How could her voice sound so calm, Ashleigh wondered, when every inch of her was shaking with terror? Jilly galloped up alongside.

"I'm right here!" Jilly called over the sound of pounding hooves. "Hold her till we're around the back-stretch. At the quarter pole, open her up."

Ashleigh was too dazed to understand clearly. Where was the quarter pole? Would she have any control over Wonder when they got there? All she could think about now was staying in the saddle. The horses were flying, yet the track seemed endless. She'd never get around. Wonder would fly off across the track, jump the railing. They'd both be hurt or killed. *Don't bolt, Wonder,* Ashleigh prayed. *Just a little longer and you can go, Wonder.* Already Ashleigh's arms ached from trying to hold back one thousand pounds of powerful horse. The reins were getting slippery from sweat. Ashleigh's legs felt like rubber.

They swept around the turn off the backstretch. Suddenly she heard Jilly shout, "Let her out!"

Numb and terrified, Ashleigh automatically eased her hands forward, giving Wonder more rein and the signal to open up. Jilly and Dominator had jumped into the lead. Ashleigh readied herself for the added burst of speed from Wonder. But nothing happened.

Wonder didn't quicken her pace. If anything, she started to slow.

Ashleigh didn't understand. For an instant, she was totally stunned. And then, in a flash, she realized what

*147*

it must be. Wonder was remembering other clockings on the track. This was the point when Jocko went to his whip. And once Wonder felt the whip, she refused to perform.

Ashleigh had to make the horse *want* to run—and run her heart out. If she didn't, Wonder would do the same thing every time she got on a track. "I'm not going to whip you!" Ashleigh cried. "There's nothing to be afraid of. Come on! Do it for *me*, then. Don't let Dominator beat you!" Ashleigh kneaded her hands along the length of Wonder's neck, urging her to more speed. "Run, girl!"

Wonder was listening now. Her ears were back, tuned to Ashleigh's pleading voice. Ashleigh could almost feel the filly's indecision. Then Wonder grunted.

"Go!" Ashleigh cried. "You can do it! That's it! That's the way!" Gradually Ashleigh felt the change. Wonder began to put her heart into it and stretch out. Dominator and Jilly were lengths ahead of them, but Ashleigh could see the gap begin to close. Wonder had made up her mind to run. All Ashleigh needed to do was keep her on the rail, prevent her from running out in a straight line on the turn. They thundered past Charlie and Linda. Ashleigh tried to see ahead. Wonder's mane blew back into her face, stinging her eyes. She knew they were gaining on Jilly and Dominator. Then she saw Dominator's flank.

Wonder stretched out further. By the time they

passed the pole marking the end of the half mile, Wonder had her nose in front and was still turning on the speed.

"Ease up! Whoa, girl!" Ashleigh cried. "You've done it! Good girl! Good girl! That's it," Ashleigh gasped as the filly finally dropped her speed. "You got over being afraid of the whip! You can run on the track again. They haven't ruined you. Oh, Wonder, I know you're going to race. I know it!"

She patted Wonder's neck, and the filly picked up her legs and arched her neck proudly at Ashleigh's praise. As they cantered back around the track, Ashleigh realized she was trembling again—but this time in relief and happiness.

Jilly looked worried as she trotted up to meet them. "You okay?" she asked Ashleigh. "What happened back there? Why did you slow her down so much? *How* did you? I thought for a while that nothing could stop her."

"I didn't slow her. She slowed down herself as soon as we came to the quarter pole and I asked her to go." Ashleigh explained the conclusions she'd come to.

"Aha. Sure, I bet that's it. She thought she was going to get smacked. But she made up for it, didn't she?"

"You think the time was good?" Ashleigh asked.

Jilly laughed. "Yeah, I think it was good. Old Dominator thought he was back in stakes races again with the big runners!"

"You two gave me a couple more gray hairs for a while there." Charlie grinned as they rode toward him. He looked up at Ashleigh. "I heard what you and Jilly were saying. She balked as soon as you asked her to go. I saw her do the same thing when she was training with Jennings. She'd drop right back in the pack at the first sign of a whip. Trying to tell him she didn't want any part of it. But the good news is that you got her going. She knows she can run the track now without getting stung."

"What was our time, Charlie?" Ashleigh couldn't wait any longer.

"Not bad," Charlie said, suddenly serious. "Considering."

"Not bad?" Linda burst in. "The half in forty-four and three-eighths. And she did the second quarter *faster* than the first!"

Ashleigh stared. With their slow start, she'd never expected Wonder to make up that much time. Ashleigh looked to Charlie for confirmation.

"Yup," he said. "And she was picking up speed all the way. She gave Dominator a run for his money all right." Charlie's eyes were twinkling like blue sparklers. "We'll keep working to break her of that habit of slowing at the turn. But today was a good start. I'd say in two weeks she'll be ready to let Maddock take a look."

"Two weeks?" Ashleigh said. "Did you hear that,

girl? We're going to show them how good you are—just like we said." But even as Ashleigh spoke, she felt a pang of uneasiness. If Maddock was impressed with Wonder, would Ashleigh's days of riding the filly be over?

"Who's that?" Jilly said suddenly.

"Where?" the others asked.

Jilly pointed to the trees near the oval. "I saw somebody running out from under the trees and heading for the stable. I couldn't see who it was."

"Are you sure?" Linda asked. "It's pretty dark to see anyone."

For the first time that night, Charlie scowled. "Hmph. We may not have a secret anymore."

Yet for the next two nights, no one disturbed their training sessions on the oval. Jilly told them that none of the stable hands had said anything about seeing them training Wonder. And with the excitement of Wonder's improvement on the track, they soon forgot about the mysterious observer.

With Ashleigh's kind treatment, Wonder was overcoming her fear of the track. She settled down and concentrated during the gallops they gave her, listening to Ashleigh and trying to do the right thing. She'd stopped associating the track with the whip, and was running the way she was born to.

Charlie was almost jolly, he was so pleased. "I can't

wait to see their faces when they get a load of these timings." He chuckled.

When Ashleigh went off to school Monday morning, she was feeling on top of the world. She and Linda sat down at lunch together as usual.

"Boy," Ashleigh said, "I didn't realize how hard it is to gallop a couple of miles around a track. It's not the same as galloping on the trails. You need so much more stamina and strength."

"You've gotten a lot better the last couple of nights. Going out on the track was good training for you, too."

"Do you think? I *feel* like I'm getting better—I know what to do now and don't get so scared when something goes wrong." Ashleigh frowned for a second. "But I don't think I'm as good as some of the other riders yet—definitely not as good as Jilly. Tell me the honest-to-God truth, Linda. Do you think I'm as good —or almost as good—as Brad? You watched him on the track the other morning."

Linda thought for a moment. "You don't ride the same. He's got a whole different technique. He uses muscle and rides hard."

"I know. But say he and I were out on the track together—do you think I could keep Wonder going well enough to beat him and Townsend Prince?"

Linda laughed. "The horses have something to do with it too, you know. Townsend Prince is fast—but so is Wonder." Linda considered. "Brad's got more experience, but I'd say that if the horses were equal, you'd get more out of Wonder the way you ride."

Ashleigh chewed a fingernail, not quite satisfied. "I look okay when I'm out there? I don't look like I'm sitting in the saddle like a sack of grain, letting Wonder do all the work?"

"No, Ash! Will you stop worrying?" Linda smiled. "Besides, I can't imagine any other rider—except for maybe Jilly—getting Wonder to go like you do. Now, look at this race schedule for Churchill Downs. I borrowed it from my father's office. I was trying to find some good maiden two-year-old races for Wonder. What do you think?"

Ashleigh took a bite from her sandwich and studied the schedule. "Hmm. But we're really planning ahead, aren't we?"

"My mother always tells me to think positive."

"Right," Ashleigh agreed with a grin.

Jennifer suddenly slid into the seat next to Ashleigh. "Your sister's still going out with Brad, isn't she?" she said in a wistful voice.

"Yeah." Ashleigh didn't want to talk about Caro and Brad. She reached for her juice carton and drained it, even though she wasn't thirsty.

"God, she's so lucky. He's gorgeous."

"You think so?" Ashleigh said.

"I saw him at Keeneland last fall in the winner's circle with his father. How did your sister do it?"

"We live on the same farm. Now that she's started pretending she's interested in horses, she sees him all the time. Ask her." Ashleigh crumpled up her juice carton. "I'm going to walk around outside before lunch hour's over. You want to come, Linda?"

Both girls started to rise, but Jennifer's voice broke in. "I was going to ask you, Ash. I've been dying to see Townsend Acres. Could I come over one afternoon . . . and maybe you could show me around?"

Ashleigh studied Jennifer, with her brilliant blue eyes and blond mane. She hadn't forgotten Jennifer's comment about her appearance at the dance months before. And Jennifer had never paid any real attention to Ashleigh until Caroline had started going out with Brad.

"Come over whenever you want," Ashleigh said. "But don't expect me to introduce you to Brad, because I think he's an absolute and ultimate pain in the butt."

Jennifer stared. Her mouth fell open slightly, and Ashleigh turned and walked away.

Charlie was waiting on the Griffens' front porch when Ashleigh got home—and he didn't look happy.

"We got problems," he said brusquely.

Ashleigh stared at him, then suddenly felt frightened. "What? Tell me!"

"Maddock talked to me today. Seems Jilly did see somebody watching us train on the track—one of the grooms, Hank. Darned snitch. I don't know why he couldn't come to me first, but he waited till Maddock got back this morning. Hank saw the whole shooting match, including that final breeze. He's no slouch. He knew the kind of time she was clocking. Now Maddock wants to see her work himself—tomorrow morning."

Ashleigh's first reaction was elation. Then her heart fell. "But she's not ready, is she, Charlie? And who's going to ride her? Did Maddock say? Is he going to let me? Oh, no, but I have school! What about Jilly?"

"Whoa," Charlie said, cutting her breathless questions short. "I'm not sure what Maddock is going to do yet. The groom didn't tell him you were riding the filly that night, and I didn't know if it was smart to mention it to him—you know, me letting a young kid gallop a green horse on the track. All right," Charlie said quickly when he saw Ashleigh's face, "I know you're good enough, but Maddock has to think about spills and insurance. Anyway, he said he thought we weren't going to do any more than ride the filly around the trails over the winter—keep her fit. He didn't know we were working her at training level."

"He was mad?"

"I think he might have been if he hadn't been so curious to see what Hank was talking about."

"If he won't let me ride, did you ask him if Jilly could?"

"I mentioned it—tried to explain how we'd turned the horse around with different handling. I don't think he took me seriously. He doesn't think the horse could have improved that much—that Hank was imagining things. But Townsend was there when Hank told him about Wonder, and Townsend's the one who wants to see her run."

"Oh, no," Ashleigh moaned. "Then it's really important she does well."

"Yup. I won't argue with you there."

"What are we going to do, Charlie?" Ashleigh worried.

"I don't see as we have any choice except to do what Maddock says and get the filly out there to the track early tomorrow morning. But I want to get some work in this afternoon—you can bet on that!"

"I'll go change and meet you at the barn," Ashleigh said, already heading for the door.

Charlie and Ashleigh were so concentrated on the workout, they barely noticed anything else. The horses sensed that something was happening. Wonder and Dominator were both incredibly alert and ready to start dancing on their toes at the slightest provocation. Charlie was riding Dominator, since Maddock had given Jilly other work to do that afternoon.

They'd cantered and lightly galloped the two horses over the hilly ground. Now Charlie wanted to breeze Wonder for a short distance down the lane. "You won't be able to time her," Ashleigh said as they came onto the lane.

"I don't want to work her too hard," he said, frowning. "She has to be fresh in the morning. But I want her ready—not dozing from too little exercise."

Ashleigh nodded. Wonder was performing like an angel—ready to do anything. But would she do the same in the morning?

"What worries me," Charlie said, "is that she hasn't been breezing with a bunch of other horses yet. She did last fall, but we might as well write off anything she learned then."

"She's been running with Dominator," Ashleigh said.

"Yeah. She knows him. But he won't be out there. It'll be a bunch of strange horses. She might go back to being contrary—slowing down and running with the pack just out of habit. I'll talk to Jilly later." Charlie shook his head.

They finished the workout with a light gallop down the lane. Neither of them pushed the horses—Charlie had given Ashleigh strict instructions not to. But even without any prompting from Ashleigh, Wonder kept her nose in front of Dominator. If Dominator speeded up, Wonder did too—on her own.

Ashleigh looked over at Charlie, expecting him to be pleased. He looked worried.

There were more curious faces than usual watching them as they rode through the stable yard on the way to the barn. Ashleigh barely noticed. She did see Caro, talking to Brad.

When Ashleigh had untacked Wonder, cooled her down, and brought her back to her stall, Caroline came up to the stall door, alone.

Caroline didn't say anything for a few minutes. She just watched silently as Ashleigh carefully brushed Wonder's silky and gleaming coat.

"She's definitely a beauty," Caroline said finally.

Wonder looked up from her feed tray and nickered. Ashleigh only nodded. She had a funny feeling that she knew what was coming.

"Brad told me they're going to try Wonder tomorrow morning," Caroline said. "Ash, please don't be mad at me for saying it—"

"Don't bother." Ashleigh swept the brush down Wonder's back. The filly's muscles rippled in pleasure. "I know what you're going to say. Brad doesn't think Wonder stands a chance against the other horses. He thinks she'll start running with the pack when she gets out there."

"Well, yeah. I just don't want you to be hurt. I mean, maybe you don't like Brad very much, but he does know horses. You've worked hard and you love Wonder, but maybe she isn't ever going to be a great racehorse. That doesn't mean she's not a nice horse. . . ."

Ashleigh felt her anger rising. She took a deep,

steadying breath. She shouldn't get mad at Caroline. She shouldn't yell. Caroline thought she was helping. Caroline really didn't understand. Caroline was in love and thought Brad and all his opinions were special— she wasn't thinking straight.

"She'll be okay, Caro," Ashleigh said stiffly. "I still believe in her, and so does Charlie. And if she doesn't do well, then that's that, isn't it?"

"I just thought I'd talk to you," Caroline said in an almost pitying voice.

"Thanks," Ashleigh answered shortly.

Ashleigh finished feeding and grooming Wonder. She forced Caro's comments from her mind and tried to build up Wonder's confidence instead. "You'll show them, Wonder. I know you can."

Wonder scratched her head affectionately against Ashleigh's shoulder.

"If only I could ride you, though!" Ashleigh added a moment later. "Then I'd be sure, girl. I know we could do it!"

The horse nickered. Ashleigh didn't tell Wonder that she was scared.

Yet while she'd been with Wonder, she'd made up her mind. She had to be there in the morning to watch the workout. She couldn't desert Wonder now. She needed to be nearby no matter what happened. She'd go through a thousand miserable, torturous agonies if she had to be in school—not knowing. She went into the house and found her mother up in her bedroom, putting freshly folded laundry in the dresser.

"Mom, can I talk to you for a sec?"

Her mother looked up and smiled. "Sure. What's up?"

"I'd like to go to school late tomorrow. Mr. Maddock and Mr. Townsend want to see Wonder work tomorrow, and I've got to be there!"

Her mother cocked her head to the side as she listened. "So," she said, "someone was impressed with what they saw those nights you were riding on the track."

"It was supposed to be a secret!" Ashleigh gasped. How did her mother know they'd been using the track? Ashleigh had only told her parents that she was going to the stable.

"With you and Linda acting like a couple of giggling criminals, it wasn't hard to figure out what you were up to. Don't worry, your father and I didn't mind. We know you're in safe hands with Charlie and Jilly. In fact, we got a kick out of watching you keep this huge secret." She chuckled. "But it adds to the fun, doesn't it, when there's a little danger involved?"

"Oh, Mom!" Ashleigh cried. Then she started laughing too. "We were acting pretty dumb, huh?"

"Pretty obvious. You think Wonder will do well tomorrow?"

"Her clockings were so good, Charlie couldn't believe it. We've broken the bad habits she was getting. Charlie wanted to work with her a little longer before telling Maddock, but she's good—I know she is—except that they might put a rider up on her who doesn't know how to handle her. . . ." Ashleigh babbled on, explaining everything and finally running out of breath. "So, is it all right? Can I go to school late?"

"You can take the day off."

"I can!" Ashleigh jumped right off the floor in her excitement. "I don't believe it. Oh, thanks, Mom!"

"Well, anyone who can bring home a report card with honors, when a year ago they were failing, deserves a treat."

Ashleigh rushed over and threw her arms around her mother.

She called Linda right after dinner to tell her what had happened.

"Well, I know my parents aren't going to let me take a day off." Linda sighed. "I'll be thinking about you and Wonder. Good luck, Ash. It would be so great if you could ride her, though."

"I know."

Ashleigh went to bed early, knowing that she'd have to get up at four. But she couldn't sleep. She thought of everything that could possibly happen in the morning. They wouldn't let Jilly ride. Wonder would get nervous, act up, and throw Jilly. Wonder would run out. She'd get mad at Ashleigh for not riding her and sulk.

The sheets were a tangled mess from her tossing and turning. Ashleigh had to think of something good or she'd never get to sleep. She remembered the racing schedule Linda had showed her. She pictured Wonder in her maiden race, galloping to the lead, fighting off the challenge of another horse, thundering down the stretch, getting her nose in front, then her head, then charging forward, letting her challenger eat her dust—crossing the finish line five lengths in the lead.

By the time she'd gotten Wonder to the winner's circle, Ashleigh was asleep.

## 13

A DIM LIGHT WAS FILTERING IN THROUGH THE HIGH BARN WIN-
dows. Most of the horses were awake, hungry, and beginning to stamp impatiently in their stalls, awaiting
their morning meal. The regular grooms would be there
soon. Wonder pranced in her stall and gave one of the
thick-boarded walls a kick for good measure. She knew
something was up—that this morning was different
from others.

Ashleigh slipped inside the stall. With another horse,
she might have hesitated. But she had no fears of Wonder—except when she was on Wonder's back and the
filly was in a willful mood. It looked like Wonder was
in a willful mood today.

"Hello, girl," Ashleigh said quietly. She caught Wonder's bobbing head and kissed the horse's nose. Then
she rubbed her hand gently down Wonder's neck. "Just
calm down. Maybe if I get you your breakfast, you'll

feel better. You look like my father before he's had his coffee in the morning." Ashleigh left the stall, went to the feed room, and filled Wonder's bucket. She was hungry and dug right in.

As Wonder ate, Ashleigh studied her, admiring as usual the horse's sleek body and elegant lines.

Wonder looked up. Her brown eyes, with their delicate spray of incredibly long lashes, watched Ashleigh intelligently.

Ashleigh noticed the look. "You know I'm thinking about you, don't you? You're so beautiful. But you've got to be more than beautiful today. You're going to have to run. Oh, Wonder, I want to ride you today. Jilly can do it, I know, and you like her. But I have this horrible feeling . . ."

Suddenly the barn seemed alive with voices. The grooms had arrived—and Ashleigh heard Charlie's gruff tones too. The horses stamped and cried out with demanding whinnies. A radio started blaring. A DJ predicted a lousy weekend ahead, and then a loud rock tune echoed around the barn. The horses whinnied louder, and someone quickly turned down the volume.

"You got your riding clothes on," Charlie said when he reached Wonder's stall and came inside.

"Just in case," Ashleigh answered. "Did you talk to Jilly?"

"She asked Maddock if she could ride the filly, but he told her he hadn't figured out his schedule yet. She's exercising a lot of horses for him—a couple that are doing good at the track and will be racing soon," Charlie said. "He told her he'd let her know this morning, and I haven't seen her yet."

That wasn't what Ashleigh wanted to hear. She needed to know for sure that Jilly was riding Wonder. Her palms felt clammy as she started tacking up the filly. Charlie quickly gave her a hand.

"Won't do any good to work yourself into a state," he said.

"Aren't you worried, Charlie?" Ashleigh protested.

"Yeah," he acknowledged as he buckled the chin strap on Wonder's bridle. "I'd be lying if I said I wasn't. All that work, and she was doing so good. She's high strung this morning, too," he added as Wonder started prancing impatiently. "Real playful—which is fine, if she's got the right rider in the saddle."

"You're not making me feel any better, Charlie," Ashleigh moaned.

"Ignore my muttering," he said as they led Wonder from the barn. "She'll be okay."

But by the time they reached the stable yard, Ashleigh felt physically sick from worry. She looked over at the training oval and saw the trainers and Mr. Townsend standing near the opening to the track, talking with some of the riders who were already mounted. Townsend was taller than the trainers and was wearing a sports jacket and tie. He looked so businesslike—and so important.

She tried to see if Brad was around, working Townsend Prince. She finally saw him, out on the track. He was riding toward the gate where his father and the trainers stood. *Why does he have to be here?* Ashleigh thought. She desperately wanted to prove him wrong—prove to him that Wonder could do well. But anything might happen that morning.

As Ashleigh, Charlie, and Wonder neared the track entrance, one of the grooms came running over.

"Hello, Hank," Charlie said coldly. "Thanks for going behind my back and talking to Maddock."

The small, dark-haired man laughed. "Doing you a favor, Charlie. The filly can run."

"Who's riding her?" Charlie asked.

"What's it matter?" the groom said. "If she's good, she's good."

"She needs the right kind of rider. Is Maddock putting Jilly up?"

"I don't know who's riding this horse." Hank shifted his glance, refusing to look Charlie in the eye. Ashleigh could practically see the black clouds gathering in Charlie's own eyes.

Then Ashleigh heard her name called. She looked up and saw Jilly riding toward them. Jilly was pale and upset.

"Ashleigh, I'm sorry!" Jilly cried. "Maddock

wouldn't let me ride her. He wants me to work Bow Ridge, since I've been riding him at the track. I've got to take him out on the trails."

Ashleigh stared at Jilly as her news sank in. "But, then—who's riding Wonder?"

Jilly shook her head and started to speak, but Maddock called her. She gave Ashleigh one last sad look before riding over to the trainer.

Wonder suddenly jerked up her head and gave a whinnying cry of distress. Ashleigh had all she could do to calm her. "Easy, girl," she said as she held firmly to Wonder's bridle.

"Full of it, isn't she?" a voice said. Ashleigh spun around and saw Jocko walking up to them. No wonder Jilly had looked so upset—no wonder the filly was jumping out of her skin!

"You're riding her?" Ashleigh cried.

Jocko grinned. "Why sound so surprised? It's not like I haven't ridden her before."

Hank grabbed Wonder's reins from Ashleigh and held the startled horse's head. Jocko boosted himself into the saddle. Wonder's nostrils flared wide. She laid her ears back flat against her head.

"You can't ride her!" Ashleigh shouted.

"Oh, yeah?" Jocko laughed. "Watch me. It's time she had a decent rider on her back." With that he kicked Wonder forward onto the track. Wonder was fighting him every inch of the way. She kicked out her heels, fought his tug on the reins, bucked; did everything she could to get her rider off her back.

Ashleigh watched in horror, but there was nothing she could do. Jocko held on and forced Wonder into a canter up the track.

Charlie had rushed over to the trainers gathered at the rail. Ashleigh ran after him. "Don't put that jock on her back!" Charlie cried. "He's no good for her. I've been training her all winter, and I know she needs a different kind of handling."

But Maddock was already giving instructions to the riders on the track. Jennings answered instead with a self-assured smile. "You've been babying her. You put a green kid up on her—that Griffen girl. What's that going to tell you about the horse? Nothing!"

"The filly's only out here today because Hank was impressed with her gallops!" Charlie shot back. "And the Griffen girl was riding her then."

"Hank was imagining things. It was dark. That filly isn't going to change her colors that fast."

"You can't get it through your head, can you?" Charlie barked, completely losing his temper. "It's the way she's ridden that makes the difference. She doesn't like rough handling!"

"The Griffen girl was riding her when Hank saw them?" Mr. Townsend interrupted.

"Yes," Charlie answered. "And the girl knows how to handle the filly. Jilly does too. The filly responds to it."

Ashleigh stared at the men, holding her breath. She quickly looked over to where Jilly had been standing with her mount. But Jilly was gone. Maddock had sent her out on the trails.

"Interesting," Townsend said. "But it's too late to change riders now. Let's just see how she does. I can't see how a rider's going to make that much difference. Either she's got speed or she doesn't."

Ashleigh's heart sank to her feet. "It will make a difference," she whispered. But if the men wouldn't listen to Charlie, they sure wouldn't listen to her. Numbly she looked out to the track.

Maddock had sent Wonder out with three other two-year-olds—three of the best in training. The horses were already galloping down the backstretch, approaching the turn where the clocking would start. Wonder was staying with the others, but Ashleigh could see that Jocko was still hand-riding her. He hadn't gone for his whip yet.

Ashleigh couldn't breathe. The men had stopped arguing and were all staring at the track as well. Ashleigh gripped the rail so tightly her knuckles turned white.

The horses swept around the turn. Maddock lifted his left hand. He held his stopwatch in his right. He dropped his hand. Ashleigh knew what was going to happen. Her nightmare suddenly became real as Jocko lifted his whip.

At the whip's sting, Wonder danced right across the

track, bumping into other horses. Jocko grappled with the reins, heavy-handing her back on course. He smacked her again.

Wonder's whole body shivered in distress. She'd been close to the front. Now, the other horses started moving past her—first one, then two—until she was trailing by half a length. Jocko kept fighting with her and smacking her with his whip.

Ashleigh couldn't stand to watch any longer. She closed her eyes and felt the tears sliding down her cheeks. This one ride would ruin all her and Charlie's months of work. She didn't want to see Wonder's fear and confusion and know that the filly might never trust her again for letting this happen.

She heard the horses thundering by in front of her. She listened in a daze to the hoofbeats pounding on up the track. When she finally dared to open her eyes, she saw that what she feared had come true. Wonder was trailing behind the other horses. The filly wasn't even trying. She looked just as bad as Jennings had claimed.

Charlie came up behind Ashleigh and laid a hand on her shoulder. "I haven't given up yet," he said.

Ashleigh was too choked up to speak. She could only nod as the horses turned to come off the track. Dimly, she heard Jennings's voice behind her.

"What did I tell you?" he said. "Put her in with other horses, and she backs right off. She was doing the same thing last fall. The filly's not competitive—she's a herd animal. You can't tell me a different rider's going to change her performance that much."

"She hates the whip!" Charlie cried. "Can't you see what's in front of your face? As soon as the whip comes out, she slows down."

"You're crazy," Jocko growled as he dismounted. "The filly just doesn't want to run. She'd make better dog food."

"Hold it," Mr. Townsend said.

Ashleigh was barely listening. She'd run to Wonder and was desperately trying to quiet the filly. The whites were showing around Wonder's eyes. The filly was frantic, shaking.

"I think Charlie may have a point," Townsend said. "At least I'd like to see whether or not he's right before I give up on her. I see Jilly's gone. Think the Griffen girl can handle her for a breeze?" he asked Charlie.

Ashleigh was suddenly listening with full attention. She turned, her face alight. "Yes," she gasped.

"She can ride her," Charlie said firmly.

"Have her take her out, then," Townsend told him. "These horses haven't been worked too hard. Another short breeze won't hurt them."

"It's a waste of time," Jennings sputtered.

Townsend ignored him. "I'll see that for myself."

Ashleigh saw Jocko glowering.

"Okay," Maddock said, following orders. "Let's just take them from a standing start this time. I don't want to push them too hard." The head trainer didn't look very optimistic.

Ashleigh knew that here was their chance. She fastened the chin strap of her helmet as Charlie hurried over to her and Wonder. A thousand butterflies started waging war in her stomach. She felt trembly all over. Could she do it?

"Charlie, she's all strung out," she whispered frantically. "Is she going to calm down?"

"It's the only chance we got," he said as he gave Ashleigh a leg up into the saddle. Wonder shied, but Charlie held her bridle.

"But they're all colts." Ashleigh gulped as she adjusted her stirrups, bringing them up another notch. Her legs felt like jelly. "They're bigger, and colts almost always run faster than fillies."

"Wonder can outrun them—*if* she puts her mind to it. Just take it easy with her until she realizes it's you in the saddle. Let's hope she realizes in time to do some decent running. Okay, girl, easy, easy," he said to the horse. "You do your stuff like I know you can."

Ashleigh rubbed Wonder's neck and adjusted her grip on the reins, holding them firmly, but not so tightly that the filly felt any abrasion in her mouth. "It's me up here now, girl. You know I'm not going to hurt you. You and I can do it—like we've done before."

"Ready?" Maddock called to Ashleigh.

Ashleigh dropped her heels, settled deep in the sad-

172

dle, looked over to Maddock, and nodded. The other horses were already moving out onto the track. Tightening her legs, Ashleigh urged Wonder forward. For one frantic moment she thought Wonder was going to balk, refuse to move. "Come on, girl. It's okay." Again, she squeezed the filly gently with her legs. Snorting, Wonder walked forward onto the track.

Maddock motioned that he wanted the horses to start at the quarter pole and run to the three-quarter pole. The other riders were already positioning their horses in a line. Ashleigh headed Wonder in that direction. "Let's just trot nice and easy for a while." The filly's ears flicked back, listening, but Ashleigh felt the tremors in Wonder's body.

Saying a silent prayer, Ashleigh urged the filly up to join the other riders. The filly trotted up, but as soon as Ashleigh went to turn her, she exploded into a series of bucks. She refused to go to the line. She refused to stand still. She kept veering off and shying away, whinnying shrilly in protest.

Ashleigh struggled to control Wonder, who was now trying to rear up. She didn't look at the other riders' faces, but she heard their disgusted comments. "We're wasting our time," one growled. "She can't handle that filly. Jocko's right."

Ashleigh didn't know what to do. Her gentle words weren't having any effect. Wonder stubbornly refused going to do any decent running now after getting so worked up."

"Please, wait!" Ashleigh cried. "She'll calm down." She saw Charlie signal to Maddock to give her and Wonder another minute.

Ashleigh leaned over Wonder's neck, as close to the filly's ears as she could. "Please, Wonder, please. Don't you understand? Your whole future depends on whether you run. You've got to calm down. Can't you do that for me? Please . . . for both of us, Wonder?" As she spoke, she rubbed the filly's neck. "It's me, Wonder. You always do it for me. Come on."

Wonder trembled, but Ashleigh's words were finally getting through the filly's panic. Wonder shuddered, but stopped veering. Then slowly, she came to a halt.

"Good girl, good girl," Ashleigh praised breathlessly. "Let's just move up in line with the others. You know, like you and Dominator do all the time. Then we're going to run—run the way you love to."

Wonder whuffed uneasily. Her ears were pricked back now, concentrated on Ashleigh's voice. At Ashleigh's coaxing, she walked forward. Ashleigh stopped her alongside the other horses and kept talking. "Easy —easy. We're going to do this, girl. There's nothing to be afraid of." At the same time Ashleigh watched Mad-

174

dock, waiting for his signal. She prayed it would come soon. She heard one of the other riders sniggering. She didn't know how she could keep the trembling filly calm and alert.

Maddock's arm fell. Ashleigh instantly tightened her legs and gave Wonder rein. "Go!" she cried. "Run, Wonder! Run like you always do. Run your heart out!"

Wonder hesitated for the briefest instant, then suddenly she jumped out with a powerful leap. Ashleigh leaned forward over the filly's neck, moving with Wonder's stretching body, losing herself in the rhythm of the forceful strides, feeling Wonder's muscles smoothly bunching with each stride. "Go!" she cried. "That's it, girl! That's it!"

Ashleigh couldn't think of anything now but the ride ahead. They were on the outside, in the middle of the track, with the longest distance to travel, but Wonder stayed abreast of the others. "Come on, baby!" Ashleigh whispered.

All of Ashleigh's concentration was on the filly. Ashleigh knew Wonder was eyeing the horse beside her. The filly wanted to be in front—her heart was in it. "Okay," Ashleigh whispered. "Let's beat 'em, then." Wonder found another gear. Slowly, she started moving out into the lead. The others weren't about to give up. They fought back, and one of the riders went for his whip. Ashleigh cringed—praying that Wonder wouldn't see it. But Wonder kept her nose in front.

175

The horse next to them began to tire and fall back. Ashleigh could sense Wonder's delight at having put one competitor away. But the two horses closer in to the rail were still running strong—and they had the advantage of the shorter distance around the turn ahead.

Ashleigh started moving Wonder in closer to the rail. Then, from the corner of her eye, she saw another rider go for his whip. She gritted her teeth and held Wonder out in the center of the track. She couldn't let Wonder see that whip. She'd have to take her chances with the wider distance, even though it would be harder on the filly. She had to get Wonder farther into the lead before the turn—before any flaying whips got too close to her.

Wonder didn't need Ashleigh's encouragement anymore. She stretched and got her neck in front of the horse beside her, then increased her speed again. The fence poles flashed by in a blur. Ashleigh didn't know where the filly was finding her reserves of strength—but she *was* finding them and showing no signs of tiring.

The horse beside them began falling back, but the colt on the rail hadn't given up the race. Ashleigh wondered if he was starting to tire. His strides were growing labored. "Come on, girl!" she called to Wonder. "I think we've got it. We can do it! Just get ahead of this guy before the turn."

Wonder dug in harder. The other horse started falling back. Wonder pulled them to a half-length lead—then a full length—and kept going. Ashleigh saw the pole ahead marking the end of the half mile. Wonder flew around the turn, still increasing her speed, galloping her heart out. Ashleigh was so intent on staying in the lead, she didn't even see the pole as they passed. Wonder wasn't ready to quit yet. Ashleigh suddenly realized, as they started pounding down the backstretch, that they'd gone much too far. She had to slow Wonder down. She couldn't let her run flat out for such a long distance. The strain would be too much for her!

Ashleigh dragged back on the reins and stood in the stirrups. "Whoa, girl, whoa!" Wonder understood the signals, but she wasn't ready to stop. She still had more to give.

They were halfway down the backstretch. Ashleigh pulled on the reins until her hands felt raw. "Whoa! You've got to slow down!" She stood as tall as she could in the stirrups, pulling hard on the reins. Wonder fought against the pressure. "Don't run away with me now, Wonder!" Ashleigh pleaded. "You've done such a good job."

At last, near the end of the backstretch, Wonder started to slow. She tossed her head and snorted her disappointment at being stopped.

Ashleigh was finally able to turn the cantering filly. She rubbed her hand over Wonder's neck. "Oh, girl, you scared me out of my mind for a while," she gasped excitedly. "But you were great! You're wonderful! We did it, girl!" Ashleigh cried. "We did it! You beat them! I love you! I'm so proud of you!"

Wonder arched her neck and again tossed her head so that her silky mane went flying. Ashleigh trotted back toward the other riders, who'd already turned their horses. She wasn't afraid to look at their faces now. They all looked stunned. Then one of them finally smiled. "Nice going, kid."

"Nice ride."

"Nice filly!"

The trainers looked equally stunned as Ashleigh followed the others through the gate and off the track. Jennings had stepped a few feet back behind the others. He not only looked embarrassed, but worried. Jocko stood for a few seconds glaring at Ashleigh and Wonder with a red face, then turned and strode off toward the stables.

Mr. Townsend, though, was grinning. And behind him, Ashleigh saw Brad. His eyes were nearly bugging out of his head. *I told you,* she thought gleefully. *Now tell my sister about this!"*

Charlie rushed over as Ashleigh stopped Wonder. He had his hat in his hand, and it looked more crumpled than ever. He slammed it down on his head. "That was some kind of ride." He patted Wonder's steaming shoulder almost too vigorously. "Darn, but you showed them your stuff—just like I knew you could!"

Wonder twisted her head around and picked up the

brim of Charlie's hat with her lips. Charlie grabbed it away. "It's already been beaten on enough this morning. Besides, I got a better treat for you than that." He crushed his hat back on his head and dug in his pocket for a carrot.

Wonder nickered her appreciation.

"Yeah, you deserve it, too."

Ashleigh leaned down and wrapped her arms around Wonder's neck. She felt the wetness on her cheek and realized that she was crying—from sheer happiness. "You're going to be great, girl! You're going to be great!"

Clay Townsend strode over. "Charlie, I have to admit you've done incredible things with this filly. That's what I like to see!" he said. "She ran that half in unbelievable time. Looks like we've got something here after all!" He, too, laid a congratulatory hand on Wonder's shoulder and studied the horse. "I want her to go back into regular training, with the thought of starting her racing this summer." He hesitated for the briefest second, then smiled. "And I'd like you to take her over from here on out, Charlie—be her regular trainer."

Charlie readjusted his hat. "Be glad to."

"Good," Townsend said. "And I think Ashleigh'd better keep exercise riding her." He looked at Ashleigh. "Unless you have some objections."

"Me?" Ashleigh gasped, hardly believing what she was hearing. "No—I'd love to ride her. It's what I've always wanted!"

"Glad to hear it. You've both done some nice work here. I'm looking forward to a future with this filly."

As he walked off, Charlie and Ashleigh exchanged a look of amazement. "Well, I'll be!" Charlie said. "He wants me to train her. And, missy, your dream's coming true. You hear that, Wonder, girl? Looks like we're going to be a trio for a while."

Wonder craned her head around, nudged his shoulder, and nickered contentedly.

"Oh, wow!" Ashleigh laughed. "What do you think, Charlie? Is it too soon to start dreaming about the Kentucky Derby?"

"Well, we might have to set our sights a little lower than that. But it's a possibility—it's a possibility."

Here's a sneak peek at what's ahead
in this exciting series:


# THOROUGHBRED #3

## *Wonder's First Race*


An expectant hush fell over the crowd. Ashleigh
glued her eyes to the Number Six post position—Wonder and Jilly. "You can do it, Wonder," she whispered
under her breath.

The gate doors flew open, and ten Thoroughbreds
surged powerfully out onto the dirt track. Horses and
jockeys fought for position. Wonder was off half a beat
late, and the horses to either side of her suddenly
swerved in together, blocking her path.

Ashleigh cringed and held her breath as Jilly was
forced to pull Wonder up and search for another route.
Wonder didn't like running behind horses.

**Joanna Campbell** was born and raised in Norwalk, Connecticut and grew up loving horses. She eventually owned a horse of her own and took riding lessons for a number of years, specializing in jumping. She still rides when possible and has started her three-year-old granddaughter on lessons. In addition to publishing over twenty-five novels for young adults, she is the author of four adult novels. She has also sung and played piano professionally and owned an antique business. She now lives on the coast of Maine in Camden with her husband, Ian Bruce. She has two children, Kimberly and Kenneth, and three grandchildren.